AN IDAHO CHRISTMAS

PAST AND PRESENT

ROBIN LEE HATCHER

A CHRISTMAS ANGEL

PROLOGUE

1892

*A*nnie looked with excitement at the angel in the mail order catalog. She didn't think she'd ever seen anything more beautiful in her life. And this was only an ink drawing. She could just imagine what the spun-gold hair, white satin gown, and gossamer-like wings looked like.

The front door whistled open, and a cold blast of air whipped across the room as her pa entered the house.

"Pa! Come look at this!"

"What've you got there?" Her pa, Mick Gerrard, smiled as he shrugged out of his coat and hung it on a peg near the door.

"Look at the angel. Wouldn't she be perfect on top of a Christmas tree?"

He crossed the kitchen in four strides, and his hand alighted on Annie's shoulder as he bent forward, his gaze on the catalog. "Yes, she sure would, pet. She'd be perfect, all right."

Annie glanced up at him. He looked and sounded tired, and even at her age, she knew he was worried about money. She felt a stab of guilt for wanting something like the angel when she knew

3

they couldn't afford it. And it was all her fault. If she hadn't fallen out of the hayloft—

Mick ruffled his daughter's hair as he kissed her cheek. "We'll see what we can do."

"I didn't mean I wanted you to buy it, Pa," she lied. "I just thought she was pretty."

"Well, who knows? Maybe Saint Nicholas will decide to bring you one like her."

She wrinkled her nose. "I'm too *old* to believe in Saint Nick."

Her father didn't say anything more as he nodded, then left the kitchen.

After he closed his bedroom door, Annie stared at it for a long time before returning her gaze to the catalog. Guilty or not, she *did* wish they could have the angel. Angels looked out for folks on earth. Oh, not dolls. She knew better than that. But maybe if she could get the doll, she would also get a real, live angel who could fix her legs and make her pa happy, too.

She closed her eyes and wished for those things as hard as she could.

CHAPTER 1

*J*ennifer Whitmore sighed as she stared out the sooty window. The countryside, vast and snow-covered, rolled past, the train carrying her farther and farther away from Chicago and all she'd ever known.

She tried her best not to think about what she was doing—leaving behind her comfortably familiar position at the Angel of Mercy Hospital, her comfortably familiar rooms at Mrs. Mulligan's Boarding House, her comfortably familiar courtship with Harry Reynolds.

Harry had told her she was being foolish, crazy. He'd been angry that she hadn't asked him for his opinion. But what he'd wanted was for her to ask his permission.

"What if I don't want you to go?"

Maybe Harry was right. Maybe it was crazy. But he hadn't given her any reason to stay. When she'd said those exact words to him, his eyes had widened, and he'd looked as if someone was choking off his air supply. In the end, he'd stormed out of the house without saying another word.

What had she expected him to say? I love you, Jennifer. Stay and marry me, Jennifer.

No, she hadn't expected him to say he loved her. Not then and not ever. Harry had been content to see her on Tuesday and Thursday evenings at six o'clock. On Sundays, he'd never failed to walk her to and from church, three blocks from the boarding house. He'd never shown any inclination to deviate from his accustomed routine, certainly not with such a drastic step as marriage.

What would she have done if Harry had proposed? She supposed she was relieved he hadn't. Whenever she'd tried to imagine herself as his wife, she'd failed. She was no more in love with him than he was with her. Even an old maid had a few dreams left. Even she wanted her heart to experience flights of ecstasy.

She closed her eyes. When she did, it wasn't Harry's face that came to mind. It was a face from the past. A face she often remembered. A face she would be seeing again by this time tomorrow.

How much would Mick Gerrard have changed since she'd last seen him? Would his hair be the same honey-brown? Would it still be thick and unruly, the way she remembered it? Would his eyes be the same intense shade of blue, like the sky on the clearest of winter days? Would he still stand head-above-the-crowd tall? Would he have that same crooked smile that used to make her heart flip-flop?

She opened her eyes and straightened, shaking her head to rid herself of Mick's image. It wasn't seemly of her to think about him this way. After all, she wasn't a love-struck thirteen-year-old any longer. She was twenty-four and a trained nurse. And Mick Gerrard wasn't an eighteen-year-old clerk in her father's mercantile. He was her stepsister's widower. His daughter was her niece —and Annie Gerrard was the sole reason Jennifer was headed to Idaho.

With the sound of the train speeding along the tracks echoing in her ears, her thoughts returned to a recent Saturday night supper at her father's home.

≈

"WE NEVER SHOULD HAVE LET Annie stay out west after Christina died," Dorothea Whitmore, Jennifer's stepmother, said the moment her husband finished reading Mick's letter.

Jennifer's father, David, laid the letter from Idaho on the table near his supper plate.

Dorothea continued, her voice rising, "We should have demanded that he bring our grandchild to us immediately after the funeral. We should have known he couldn't take proper care of her. Now she's crippled. And he has the nerve to ask us for help. We shall *not* send him any money. Dear heavens, Christina's daughter a cripple. How will she ever find a proper husband when she comes of age?"

"She's a child, Dorothea," David answered his wife. "Besides, the letter doesn't say she won't get well. The doctor seems to have hope for recovery if she has the proper care."

Dorothea dabbed at her misty eyes with her handkerchief. "Oh, my poor Christina. When I think of what she had to suffer with that man. Oh, my poor, dear Christina. We shouldn't have let her marry him, no matter what she wanted. He was never good enough for her."

"Father?" Jennifer said softly. "May I see the letter, please?" She held out her hand, and he gave it to her.

Annie is in need of a nurse ... no promise that she'll walk again, although the doctor has hope ... all savings depleted ... grateful for whatever you can do...

She read the brief letter several times before she looked up again. "I'll go to Idaho to care for Annie."

"Jennifer, are you sure?"

"Yes. I'm quite sure."

~

JENNIFER'S THOUGHTS returned to the present and her gaze turned out the train window again.

Am I sure? Nerves fluttered in her stomach. No, she wasn't sure. She wasn't sure at all. But she was going, all the same.

She closed her eyes and remembered the last time she'd seen Mick. It had been his wedding day. His and Christina's. Jennifer and her father and stepmother had stood on the steps of the church and watched as the newlyweds drove off in a buggy, headed for the train depot and a new life out West.

Even after all these years, she could still feel the breaking of her young heart. Yes, it had been a schoolgirl's affection for an older boy, but it had hurt all the same, to be passed over for her much prettier stepsister. The tension in the Whitmore household prior to the wedding had added to her pain. She hadn't understood why her stepmother was angry and her father grim, why the wedding came about in such a rush.

A sigh escaped Jennifer. It was pointless to dredge up the past. It couldn't be altered. All that mattered now was helping Mick and Christina's daughter to walk again. That was her sole purpose for going to Idaho, and she had best remember it.

CHAPTER 2

*M*ick lifted Annie from the wheelchair and laid her on the bed, then pulled the blankets up snug beneath her chin.

"What's Aunt Jennifer like, Pa?"

It wasn't the first time she'd asked that question, and his answer wasn't much different from the ones he'd given before. "Don't know, pet. Last time I saw her, she was only a few years older than you. Still just a little girl. She used to hide in the storeroom and read. She loved her books more than anything back then. And I remember her telling me she wanted to be a nurse when she grew up, and that's just what she did, too."

"Is she going to be able to make my legs better?"

Mick pushed Annie's dark hair back from her face. It was difficult for him to answer around the lump in his throat. "I don't know, but I hope so. She'll do her best. We all will." He leaned over and kissed her forehead. "Now you get some sleep."

"Can't I go with you tomorrow?"

"You know what Doc Jenkins said. You're not to go out in this cold weather. We don't need you takin' sick with pneumonia."

Annie let out an exaggerated sigh.

He smiled. "Save it, pet."

She flashed a grin of her own. "You always say it never hurts to try."

When she smiled like that, he could see a little of Christina in her. Annie's hair was coal black and her eyes were umber with light flecks of gold around the darker irises—so different from Christina's red hair and green eyes—but she had her mother's perfect bone structure and ivory complexion. When Annie grew up, she would be even more beautiful than Christina had been.

"Get some sleep," he repeated, bending to kiss her one more time. He snuffed the lamp, then walked out of the child's bedroom, leaving the door ajar so he could hear if she needed him in the night.

He crossed the room that served as both the kitchen and parlor of the small farmhouse. Reaching the window, he glanced outside. The blanket of snow covering the earth sparkled in the moonlight, giving everything a peaceful, serene look.

This hadn't been a peaceful place in the early years. Christina had hated the farm and their solitary life even more than she'd hated him for bringing her to it. The house had more often served as a battleground than a home. More than once, Mick had considered giving up and going back to Chicago. It was difficult enough for a man to deal with the hardships that went hand-in-hand with farming—too little rain, too much rain, too hot, too cold, insects, blight—without having to contend with so much disharmony when the work day was done.

"What's Aunt Jennifer like, Pa?"

He wondered, too. Jennifer had been a child the last time he saw her. Had his mother-in-law managed to mold her into another Christina? If so, the coming weeks wouldn't be easy ones.

Had he made a mistake, writing to the Whitmores and asking for help? It had been sheer desperation that drove him to write that letter, and he'd regretted mailing it many times. Doing so had been a risk. If Dorothea Whitmore ever learned the truth about

Annie—that Mick wasn't her natural father, that Christina had lied, to him, to her parents, to everyone—Dorothea might be able to take Annie away from him. That he couldn't bear. That he wouldn't allow.

But he still needed help. He couldn't give his daughter the care she needed. He was just managing to hold on to the farm as it was, and since Annie's accident, what little money he'd put aside was gone. It was clear his daughter needed a nurse, and he had no way to pay for one.

He'd hoped his in-laws would cover the cost of nursing care. Instead, they were sending Christina's stepsister to care for Annie. Was it a mistake to let Jennifer come? What if she were to learn the truth and disclose it to her stepmother? What if—?

Mick shook off the questions. He had enough to worry about without borrowing trouble from tomorrow.

He turned from the window and sat at the table, his gaze focusing on the catalog, still open to the page Annie had shown him earlier. He pulled the catalog toward him. How nice it would be if he could buy that angel for her. He would like to spoil her. At least a little. Especially now.

A surge of love swept through him, just as it had on the day Annie was born. It didn't matter that Christina had played him for a fool. Not then. Not now. Nothing mattered except the love he felt for Annie Gerrard. His daughter. On the day of her birth, he'd promised God he would be the best father possible.

So help me, I'll keep that promise, Lord. No matter what.

CHAPTER 3

*J*ennifer freshened herself as best she could in the passenger car's water closet, but she saw little improvement in the chipped mirror. Her straight, pale hair was dull and in need of a good washing. Her eyes had dark circles beneath them, evidence of her sleeplessness. Her gray shirtwaist was wrinkled and travel-stained. She looked like a woman who'd been on a train for too many hours—which was what she was.

She drew herself up straight and shot a determined glance at her reflection. *It doesn't matter in the least what you look like. You're here to nurse an injured child. You're here to use your training to help her get better.*

Summoning courage and determination, she opened the door and returned to her seat. She managed to maintain her resolute posture until the conductor came through the car.

"Nampa station, next stop."

Her heart jumped into her throat. Her hands tightened in her lap. She felt the blood draining from her face, and she knew she must be as pale as a ghost. She forced herself to take several deep, steadying breaths. It wouldn't do for her to pass out from lack of oxygen and miss getting off the train.

With a screech of iron wheels against iron tracks, the Oregon Short Line pulled into the Nampa station. As soon as the train came to a complete stop, Jennifer picked up her traveling case and reticule, then rose from her seat. She drew in one more deep breath before turning toward the exit at the rear of the car. Then, with battling alley cats of nerves twisting her insides, she walked down the aisle.

MICK WAITED with his back against the train depot's wall. A bitter December wind whipped small eddies of snow across the platform, stinging exposed flesh. From beneath the brim of his weathered felt hat, he watched the passengers disembark. It wasn't as hard to find Jennifer as he'd feared it might be. Only three people got off the train, an older couple and a young woman. Clearly, the young woman had to be Jennifer.

But when he stepped forward and she turned toward him, he knew he couldn't have missed her even if there'd been a hundred other people disembarking. Jennifer Whitmore had scarcely changed from the girl he remembered sitting on a pickle barrel in her father's store, her blond hair in braids, a book in her lap. Not that she didn't look every inch a woman. She definitely did. But she still had the same large eyes—not quite blue, not quite green— and a familiar, almost waif-like expression on her delicate face.

"Hello, Mick."

"Hello, Jennifer. Look at you. I guess I was looking for a kid in pigtails, but you've grown up."

"That's what happens to a girl in eleven years." She glanced past his shoulder, then met his gaze again. "You came alone?"

"Annie's not supposed to be out in the cold."

"Of course not."

He stepped closer, reaching to take her traveling case. It was large and heavy, and he wondered how she'd managed to carry it. Although she was tall for a woman, he figured she couldn't weigh more than a hundred and ten pounds. A strong gust of wind could have blown her away.

"Come on. Let's get you out of this weather." He took her arm and guided her toward the flatbed wagon sitting on runners. He tossed her case into the back of the sleigh, then helped her onto the seat. Afterward, he hopped up beside her and handed her a lap robe. "Tuck it around you good. We've got a ways to go, and it looks like we could get more snow before we get home."

They started off to the jingle of bells and the rattle of harness.

JENNIFER HADN'T EXPECTED Mick to have changed much, but he had. He was trim, although she suspected his arms, torso, and legs were well muscled beneath the thick layer of warm clothing. His face wasn't as smooth as it had been at eighteen; trials of life had been etched into it with small lines near his eyes and mouth. His mouth. When he smiled, would his mouth be changed too? Would his smile make her feel silly inside as it used to? She clenched her hands together in her lap beneath the blanket and tried not to think such thoughts. And she tried not to think how strangely appealing the shadow of a beard beneath his skin looked. Her efforts failed. It seemed she could think of nothing else, and heat rose up her neck and flooded her cheeks.

There was no reason for either of them to feel awkward. No reason at all. They'd been friends once. He'd teased and laughed with her and even shared a few of his dreams. They could be friends again.

She drew in a deep breath. "Was the farm everything you'd hoped it would be?"

He glanced at her, a question in his eyes.

"I remember how you used to talk about it. About how you wanted a place of your own. You loved the land so much. I could tell."

He nodded, then turned back toward the road. "It hasn't been easy, but it's where I'm meant to be."

She could believe that.

"I guess it never will be easy. That's the nature of farming. It's hard work, especially when a man's got no one to depend on but himself."

Jennifer turned away. The snow-covered countryside—dotted here and there with farmhouses and silos, barns and wooden fences—seemed little different from the farmland of Illinois. If he hadn't married Christina and come west ... But he *had* married her. He *had* come west.

"I'm sorry about ... about Christina," Jennifer said. When several minutes passed without a reply, she looked in his direction. He stared straight ahead, his mouth set in a tight line, his entire body warning that she was treading on forbidden ground. Christina had been dead more than three years, but it was clear from his posture that time hadn't healed the wound of his loss. *He must still love her very much.* The thought was painful, too painful to dwell on in silence. "Tell me about Annie. What sort of child is she?"

This, at last, brought a smile. "The best. Perfect in every way."

"That's a father talking."

"She's the best. You'll see. I'm tellin' the truth."

She should have pressed him for information. She should have asked about the accident. She should have made him tell her everything the doctor had ever said or done for his patient. She should have behaved like the trained nurse she was. That was why she'd come out from Chicago, to take care of Annie, to try to make her well and whole again.

But she couldn't bear to take away Mick's smile quite so soon.

She wanted to enjoy it just a little longer. So she smiled in return and allowed them to continue on in a comfortable silence.

CHAPTER 4

$\mathcal{T}$he white clapboard house was set back from the road about a quarter mile. It was small and, if not for the green shutters framing the windows, it would have been difficult to see against the snowy fields. There was an unpainted outhouse about fifty feet off to the right. To the left was a barn, a chicken coop, and a corral for the horses. Several large trees surrounded the house. The limbs were bare now, but come spring their leafy branches would provide plenty of cooling shade. Behind the barn Jennifer saw an orchard, the fruit trees planted in neat rows.

"Apples," Mick said, seeing where her gaze had traveled. "We make a great cider."

"You do love it here, don't you?"

"That I do."

With sudden insight, Jennifer realized how it must have galled him to write to the Whitmores to ask for financial help. He was a proud man who had worked hard to provide for himself and his family. If not for Annie's accident, the Whitmores might never have heard from him again, except through Annie's letters to her grandparents which arrived several times a year. And Jennifer couldn't blame Mick for his unwillingness to contact his in-laws. Christina's mother had never tried to hide her disapproval of him.

Mick drew the sleigh to a halt close to the front door, ending her musings. The bells on the harness fell silent. One of the horses snorted and bobbed his head, then turned to look at the occupants in the wagon, as if to hurry them into the house.

"Let's get you inside, Jennifer, so I can unhitch the team before it starts to snow."

She glanced up and saw that the heavens had turned lead gray, the clouds thick and slung low to the earth. They looked different from the clouds that blew in over Chicago. She knew they weren't, but they seemed so.

"Jennifer?" Mick stood beside the sleigh, holding out his hand to her.

She rose and turned toward him. Unexpectedly, he placed his hands around her waist and lifted her to the ground. Heat rushed to her cheeks once again.

He didn't seem to notice her embarrassment. "Follow me." He released her and reached into the wagon bed for her traveling case.

As he led the way, she followed him on unsteady legs.

Seated in her wheelchair, Annie awaited them only a few feet inside the door. Anticipation was written across her face, and she watched closely as her father helped Jennifer out of her cloak.

"Annie," Mick said, "this is your Aunt Jennifer."

"Hi."

"Hello, Annie. It's good to meet you at last."

The girl wasn't anything like Jennifer had pictured in her mind. She had envisioned a miniature version of Christina, but instead, she saw a dark-eyed, black-haired pixie who resembled neither Mick nor her mother.

Annie's thoughts must have been along the same lines for she said, "I thought you'd have red hair."

"I used to wish I had hair like your mother's. It was beautiful."

18

The little girl's mouth pursed and she tilted her head to one side. "Yours is pretty like it is. It makes you look like the angel. Don't you think so, Pa?"

"What?"

"Don't you think Aunt Jennifer's hair makes her look like the angel? The one in the catalog."

Jennifer turned toward him, feeling self-conscious beneath his serious gaze.

"I think you're right, pet. She does look like the angel. Very pretty." Mick glanced at Annie and said something about putting the horses in the barn.

But Jennifer's thoughts remained on the words he'd said just before that. He thought her pretty? Jennifer Whitmore, pretty? She with her straight, pale hair—hair she'd hated because she thought Mick preferred unruly red curls. But he thought she was pretty, that she looked like an angel.

"Aunt Jennifer?"

"I'm sorry." She looked at Annie again. "What did you say?" She knew her cheeks had to be the color of ripe apples.

"You okay?"

"I … I'm afraid I've been on a train for so long, I can't seem to think straight. Perhaps you could show me to my room, Annie. We can talk while I get settled."

"Sure. Follow me." The girl spun her chair around.

Jennifer noticed that the furniture in the house had been pushed against the walls, leaving plenty of open space for Annie to get around in her wheelchair. That was good. One less thing for her to have to worry about.

"This is Pa's room," Annie announced, "but he's going to sleep in the loft while you're with us." She pushed open the door and rolled her chair through the opening.

Jennifer allowed her gaze to move over the room. It was sparsely furnished, like the rest of the house. There were no feminine touches that said a woman had once stayed in this room. Not even any photographs of Christina on the chiffonier.

It must hurt too much to look at her photograph.

She felt a hollow ache inside. But that was because she wished to help ease his troubles. Nothing more.

Her gaze stopped on the bed. Mick's bed. *I'll be sleeping in his bed.* The realization made her heart race and the heat return to her cheeks. "I should be the one staying in the loft," she said aloud.

"Pa wouldn't hear of it. There's no point in arguin' with him."

What was wrong with her? She was acting as if she had less common sense than her ten-year-old patient. It had to be because she was tired. She'd been nervous about seeing Mick again, nervous about meeting her niece, nervous about leaving Chicago and everything that was familiar. It was natural that her emotions would be a bit unpredictable. Wasn't it?

She drew a deep breath. "Perhaps we could set up a cot for me in your room."

Annie shook her head. "There's no room for a cot in there. It's too small." Her smile was disarming. "You might as well quit tryin' to change things, 'cause Pa will tell you this is where you're gonna stay."

Jennifer nodded. She remembered that Mick could be stubborn at times. Besides, what could it hurt to stay in this room and this bed? It was just a room. Just a bed. Once she had a good night's sleep, she would see how ridiculous she was being. Once she'd caught up on her rest, she would quit reacting as if she were still thirteen. That's all she needed. A bit of sleep. Then she would be herself again.

"Well, then, I suppose I should unpack. Will you help me, Annie?"

MICK WALKED TOWARD THE HOUSE, wind-blown snow stinging his

cheeks. He shrugged his coat up closer to his ears. If the past couple of weeks were any indication, it was going to be a long, cold winter. At least he had enough hay and grain to get his livestock through until spring. With luck and a bit of credit at the general store in town, he ought to be able to keep the three humans on the place fed as well.

When he opened the door, he saw Jennifer sitting at the table, Annie's chair pulled close. The tops of their heads—darkest ebony and palest yellow—were almost touching as they leaned toward each other. Jennifer held the mail order catalog in her lap while Annie pointed at items on the pages. The two of them looked up in unison, both smiling, traces of laughter lingering in their eyes.

Mick felt like the outsider, and in a flash, his distrust returned. Annie was *his* daughter, and no woman was going to come into his home and try to take her away from him. If that's what had motivated Jennifer to come to Idaho, she'd better pack that carpetbag of hers and head back to Chicago right now.

CHAPTER 5

*J*ennifer awakened by degrees. The first thing she noticed was the utter silence. It left her disoriented, unsure of her whereabouts. She half expected to feel the train start up again, to hear the constant chug-a-chug, to smell the smoke spewing from the engine's smokestack. But there was only silence.

Then she remembered. She was in Idaho. She was on Mick's farm … in his room … in his bed. Her heart fluttered, and for a few moments, as she nestled beneath the heavy quilt, she pretended she was there as Mick's bride and not his daughter's nurse. It was foolish, of course. She was no longer thirteen. She was an adult, an educated woman with a vocation, and it wasn't like her to entertain such flights of fancy.

A sigh escaped her. Flight of fancy or not, she couldn't help but wish she belonged in this house. She couldn't help wishing she were different. If only she'd been a fiery beauty like Christina, maybe this *could* have been her home and her family.

She rolled onto her side and hugged a pillow against her chest. If she'd been more like her stepsister, maybe Mick would have liked her enough to wait a few years. But she wasn't anything like

Christina, not in looks or in temperament. And she never would be.

Jennifer tossed the covers aside, ignoring the chilled air of the room as she rose from the bed and padded on bare feet to the window. She pushed aside the curtains to reveal a wonderland of white. Long icicles hung from the eaves of the house. Snow lay in deep drifts against the sides of the buildings, and tree limbs dipped low beneath the weight of the wintry blanket. The snow illumined the landscape, making it seem closer to dawn than it was.

She shivered, hugging herself as she turned from the window. Her glance fell on the bed, and she was tempted to scurry back into its waiting warmth. But she didn't want Mick to think she was a slugabed. There was much work to be done.

She broke a thin coating of ice in the pitcher and poured water into the bowl on her dressing table. Her ablutions were performed hastily. To help control her chattering teeth, she tried to set her mind on something other than how cold she was.

That *something* else quickly became *someone* else—Mick. He was even more handsome than she'd remembered him, and although worry pressed upon him, he still was ready with smiles for his daughter, he still was able to laugh. And the sound of his laughter still caused Jennifer's heart to quicken.

No, she wouldn't think about that either. Better to concentrate on Annie.

Last night she'd noticed that Mick catered to the girl. Annie had little need for her wheelchair since her father had been quick to bring her whatever she wanted or whatever he'd thought she wanted. That would have to change. Jennifer's patient must learn to do for herself. Whether that meant walking or learning new skills in a wheelchair, only God knew.

~

Mick shoved more wood into the stove, then clamped the iron door shut as crackling sounds filled the kitchen. With movements guided by habit rather than conscious thought, he measured grounds into the blue-speckled coffeepot filled with water and set it on the stove, then headed for his coat and hat which were hanging on pegs near the front door. He'd slipped his arms into his sheepskin-lined jacket when the door to his bedroom opened.

"Good morning," Jennifer said softly.

It had been many years since he'd heard a woman's voice at this hour, and he couldn't recall Christina ever greeting him that way. Not once in all the years they were married. It left him with a strange feeling. "Mornin'."

"We had a lot of new snow during the night."

"Sure did."

She tugged on the fitted sleeves of her brown dress. "I suppose we're lucky I arrived when I did."

"I suppose." He turned away. "I've got to tend to the livestock." He stepped out into the sub-zero temperature of dawn.

"I suppose we're lucky I arrived when I did."

Lucky? He wasn't so sure. Annie had taken to her Aunt Jennifer as if they'd known each other all her life. It made him wonder if she'd missed having a woman around the place. She'd been six when Christina died, but they'd gotten by well enough, just the two of them. Or so he'd thought.

"I suppose we're lucky I arrived when I did."

Lucky? No, he didn't think he was lucky to have her there. What if she were to guess the truth about Annie? Would she inform Dorothea?

"I suppose we're lucky I arrived when I did."

He jammed his hands into the pockets of his coat as he plodded through the high drifts of snow on his way to the barn. It was wrong to suspect the worst of Jennifer. She'd come to help Annie get well. Wasn't that more important to him than anything else? Would he risk his daughter's health in order to keep her to himself? No, he wouldn't. He would do whatever he had to do, risk whatever he had to risk, if it meant Annie could walk again.

He thought of Jennifer's tentative smile as she'd greeted him this morning. There was a sweetness there, a goodness that he couldn't argue against. Somehow, even now, it touched his heart, and he began to hope she was all she appeared to be.

"TELL ME ABOUT YOURSELF, ANNIE." Jennifer turned the sizzling bacon in the frying pan, then glanced over her shoulder.

"Like what?"

"What do you like to do when you're not in school or helping your father with the chores around the house?"

"Oh, that's easy. In the summer, I liked to ride Panda over to Miller's Pond and go swimming. Panda's my pony. Would you like to see her? Maybe later Pa'll take you out to the barn and show her to you."

"I'd like that. What else?"

"Pa and I used to go skating on the pond in the winter when it froze over, but I guess I won't be able to do that again."

Lord, if it's in Your will, heal this child. Let her walk again. Let her swim in the summer and skate in the winter. Show me how I can help her ... Show me how to help Mick, too.

"I like to read," Annie continued. "Pa's always liked for me to read aloud to him at night before going to bed. Mr. Miller—he's our closest neighbor—he has a big library full of books, and he lets me take as many as I want as long as I promise to take care of them."

Jennifer laughed. "I was the same way. I used to hide in the storeroom at my father's store so no one could find me and put me to work. I'd snitch an apple from the bin and climb up on the shelves and read for hours." She sat in a chair across from Annie and took hold of the girl's hand. "You know why I've come, don't you?"

"Sure. To take care of me while Pa runs the farm."

"Well ... yes, that's true. But you don't want people taking care of you the rest of your life. You'd like to be able to do things for yourself. To be able to dress yourself and to fix your own meals when you're older. And if you could, you'd like to go swimming in the pond again and ride your pony, wouldn't you?"

Annie nodded.

"That's going to take lots of hard work. Are you willing to work hard?"

She nodded again.

"The doctor thinks there is hope you can do all of that, but he can't make promises. Neither can I. Still, we want to try."

"I'll work hard, Aunt Jennifer. Really I will."

"Good." She rose from the chair. "We'll get started after break-fast." As she spoke, the scent of charred bacon filled the air. "Oh no! Breakfast!" She rushed to the stove. With a towel around the handle of the skillet, she pulled the pan from the heat. "I've ruined it."

Annie rolled her chair forward. "Don't worry, Aunt Jennifer. Pa and I are used to burned bacon. We like it that way. Honest, we do."

A deeper voice chimed in. "Annie's telling the truth. We're partial to burnt bacon."

She spun around to look at Mick, standing near the front door. "I don't believe you."

"You'd be surprised what we've learned to like to eat." He smiled. "Wouldn't she, pet?"

Annie giggled. "Pa says he's not much of a cook, but he says we haven't starved yet because of it, so he must be doin' all right."

In that moment, Jennifer fell in love with them both—and it had nothing to do with a decade-old schoolgirl's crush.

CHAPTER 6

*J*ennifer had beautiful eyes. Mick remembered the way she'd watched him as he worked in the back room of her father's store. She'd almost always been around when he was working, asking him questions, sharing her secrets, making him laugh. She'd made him feel as if he belonged —not a common feeling for an orphan boy who couldn't remember his own family.

Funny. He'd forgotten all that until now.

After hanging his coat on the peg, Mick crossed the room and sat down at the kitchen table.

"Annie, will you take this to the table, please?" Jennifer held out a plate of scrambled eggs.

Mick started to rise from the chair. "Here. Let me." The look Jennifer shot him stopped him cold.

"Annie is able to do it." Jennifer set the plate in the girl's lap.

Annie turned her chair around and wheeled it toward her father. She grinned as she set the plate on the table, pleased with herself. "Can I help with anything else, Aunt Jennifer?"

"Not right now. I think we've got everything." Jennifer carried the charred bacon on a plate in one hand and a pitcher of milk in the other as she stepped forward. She set them in the center of the table, then pulled out her chair and sat down across from Mick.

Their gazes met, and he thought again how beautiful her eyes were. And it wasn't just her eyes. She had a nice face, too. Who would have thought that scrawny little girl in pigtails would grow into such an attractive woman? And why hadn't he noticed that about her yesterday?

He was better off not noticing. The last time his head had been turned by a female, he'd found more grief than pleasure. He didn't need more complications in his life. He had enough as it was.

After Jennifer joined them at the table, Mick closed his eyes and prayed, "For this food, Heavenly Father, we are truly thankful. Amen." When he looked up, he found her watching him again, and an unfamiliar warmth spread through his chest. There was something very right about this moment, the three of them sitting at the table, the stove belching heat into the house.

His mouth flattened as his gaze dropped to the food. He wasn't about to be fooled by a pair of beguiling eyes and a sweet smile again. Jennifer was a woman and a Whitmore, and those were two good reasons not to trust her completely. He might have to accept her help with his daughter, but he would keep his guard up, all the same.

"I told Aunt Jennifer you'd take her out to meet Panda." Annie reached to fill her plate with eggs. "Will you, Pa?"

"Sure, but it'll have to be later. I've got chores to do."

"You aren't going into town again, are you?" Jennifer asked.

"No. Why?"

"There are a few things I need, and I would like to consult with the doctor as well."

Hadn't she noticed how far out the farm was from Nampa? Didn't she know when he was in town there was work not getting done back at the farm?

"I'm sorry for the extra trip, Mick. Truly. I didn't know what I would need until I ... until I met Annie."

Something about her soft reply reminded him of the time she'd asked for his help with building a birdhouse. She'd wanted a place for the birds to be safe from the tomcat that roamed the alley. Mick hadn't had the heart to say no. They'd spent every evening for two weeks working on that thing, and as he recalled now, he'd enjoyed every minute of it. She'd been a sweet-natured, quiet kid with a good heart. She never could stand to see anything or anyone hurt.

"It's important or I wouldn't ask," she added. "If you could hitch up the horses to the sleigh, I believe I could manage to get to town on my own. I don't mean to inconvenience you."

He would have to take her. Either that or feel guilty for not doing so. "If it can't be helped, it can't be helped." He rose. "If the weather holds, we'll go this afternoon."

"Thank you."

The way she looked at him drove the last of his irritation away, replacing it with a feeling he couldn't quite name. And he figured he'd best leave the house instead of trying.

ANNIE'S PA always said she saw too much for her own good. Take the way he'd acted this morning at breakfast. The way he'd talked. The way he'd looked at Aunt Jennifer.

It was plain as the nose on her face. He liked Aunt Jennifer.

I like her, too. And she's different from Ma.

Annie didn't remember much about her mother. The years had faded most of her memories, although she hadn't forgotten her mother's red hair and green eyes. She also remembered feeling like her ma didn't like her pa much. Or her either.

But Aunt Jennifer liked her. She could tell. Almost from the moment Aunt Jennifer came through the front door, Annie had known they were going to get along like two peas in a pod.

And if I like her and Pa likes her, maybe she'll stay with us and never go back to Chicago.

∽

JENNIFER SENT a covert glance in Mick's direction as the sleigh glided swiftly over the snowy ground. His coat collar was pulled up close to his ears, his shoulders hunched against the cold, but she could still see his handsome profile. He'd always been handsome. Looking at him had always made her pulse quicken.

How nice it would be to draw close to him, to slip her arm through his and snuggle close against his side. How nice to believe she belonged with him. That she belonged here for good. But she didn't belong, and she was setting herself up for heartbreak to hope she would.

To distract her wayward thoughts, she said, "I do appreciate your taking me to town again."

"Sure."

"I promise not to ask you to make a special trip for me again."

"Good."

Perhaps she should talk about something else. His daughter seemed the best choice of topics. "There is something I need to say, Mick. You've been doing too much for Annie. She's capable of doing a lot of things by herself. She—"

"What do you mean, too much? She came close to dyin' when she fell out of that barn."

"But she didn't die. She's hurt and for now she cannot walk, but she's very much alive. You need to let her act like it."

"I suppose *you* know what's best for her? You haven't even been here twenty-four hours and you already know more than anybody else. What if she can't do what you think she can?"

His outburst revealed both his concern and his love, and she wished she could put her arms around him and hold him and ... and ...

She stiffened her spine. "It won't hurt her to fail a time or two. She doesn't need you to wait on her hand and foot. She's a bright and ingenious little girl. She might have to do things a little differently than those who have two strong legs, but she'll figure out a way if you let her."

He met her gaze, his expression hard as iron. "I know my daughter better than you, Jennifer, and I'll take care of her as I see fit. I won't stand for your interference."

"Interference?" She drew back. "Is that what you call it when someone travels halfway across the country to help?"

He was a man in pain. He was afraid. But that fear seemed to be about more than his daughter's health. Jennifer wished she understood what it was that troubled him so. She wished she could help take away his worries. Isn't that why God said it wasn't good for man to be alone? Because a shared burden wasn't as heavy as one carried alone.

HAD her chin always looked this obstinate? Mick wondered. Yes, come to think of it, it had. Jennifer could be more than a little stubborn. But she'd also been sweet and giving. And whenever she'd fought tears, as he suspected she was doing now, he'd found it hard to resist giving in to her wishes.

Well, he was no longer an eighteen year old boy who could be swayed by a young girl's tears. Or a woman's either. Marriage to Christina had taught him many hard lessons. He wouldn't forget them just because Jennifer was close to crying.

So help him, he wouldn't.

CHAPTER 7

$\mathcal{B}$y the end of her second week on the Gerrard farm, Jennifer knew she never wanted to leave. The house was small, but it felt inviting. It was tight against winter drafts, and although the rooms grew cold during the night when the fire died down, they warmed quickly in the morning. As far as Jennifer was concerned, it was a perfect house in every way—and so were the people who lived in it.

Mick spent long hours seeing to the daily chores. He made repairs to the barn and the house, the ring of his hammer often sounding for hours on end. He mended harness and sharpened farm implements. He tended the animals and chopped wood for the stove. Even in the dead of winter, it was clear there was little rest for him.

Annie was also industrious. She was a bright, inquisitive child, and she worked hard on her school work, which her teacher brought by so she wouldn't fall behind the other students in her class. She was a good patient, too. Even when the physical exercises her aunt taught her were painful, she didn't complain or try to quit.

The love Jennifer felt for her niece seemed to grow stronger each day. They found shared interest in many things, especially in those things that made them laugh. She taught the girl how to bake her special recipe chocolate cake, and Annie showed her how to make her father's favorite apple cobbler. Jennifer made a new dress for Annie from fabric she'd brought from Chicago. Annie sketched a picture of the barn and horses and gave it to her aunt. Every day promised something new, and Jennifer loved every moment.

Her favorite time of day was evening because that was when Mick joined them. Suppertime discussions were never boring. Jennifer and Mick often chose opposing points of view, but their verbal sparring was good-natured. Sometimes they would talk about their childhoods in Chicago, sharing old memories of a place and time far removed from the present.

After supper was finished and the dishes washed and put away, the three of them would sit in the parlor. Mick would hold Annie in his lap while the girl read aloud. Jennifer would pause in her needlework or whatever task she'd chosen to keep her hands busy, and listen. She would watch the two of them and feel her heart tighten with love and longing.

There was no denying it. Jennifer loved them both. She'd never stopped loving Mick, she supposed, and now his daughter had taken up residence in her heart as well.

As she mulled over this truth one evening, Mick glanced up and their gazes met. She waited, wanting to see something in the depths of blue that would give her hope, wanting it so much she ached.

He was the first to look away, his gaze falling to the open book in his daughter's lap. He lifted his arm from behind Annie's back and stroked her black hair with his fingers. The gesture was sweet, an unconscious show of affection. Jennifer wished it was her hair he stroked.

She swallowed the hot tears that burned the back of her throat as she, too, looked away. She would never stop loving Mick

Gerrard and, when the time came, leaving him would shatter her heart into a thousand pieces.

That time would come much too soon. She had already seen encouraging signs of Annie's recovery. Jennifer wouldn't be needed for long. Perhaps until spring, if even that.

She swallowed again, tears blurring her vision. She wished she could dash them away but didn't want Annie to see and ask why she cried. How would she answer? With a lie? She didn't want to lie to the girl. With the truth? She didn't want Mick to know and reject her once again.

Suddenly overwhelmed by her emotions, she gathered her mending and rose to her feet. "Good night," she whispered, then hurried into the safety of her bedroom. Once inside, she leaned against the door and allowed the tears to run down her cheeks.

~

"What's wrong with Aunt Jennifer?"

Frowning, Mick replied, "I don't know. She seemed all right at supper."

"Maybe you should go ask."

"No." He shook his head. "She's got a right to her privacy."

His daughter scowled at him. "Maybe she's sick and needs the doctor."

"I doubt it, pet." He ruffled her hair. "She'd tell us if she needed to see Doc Jenkins. She's a nurse, remember?" He lifted the book from where it lay in her lap. "Finish the chapter. I want to know what's going to happen to Tom."

Annie was soon engrossed with Tom Sawyer again, but Mick couldn't seem to concentrate on the story. His thoughts kept returning to Jennifer, to the unhappy tone of her voice as she'd bid them good night. It wasn't like her. In the weeks she'd been with them, he'd grown accustomed to her cheerful disposition. Even when he made her angry—which had happened more than once—kindness prevailed. And soon she was her sunny self again.

Sunny—it was a word that described Jennifer better than any other. Her smile was as warm as a summer day. Her eyes made him think of a clear mountain lake. Her hair was like the sun itself. Her laughter was infectious, touching something deep inside him.

He glanced toward the closed bedroom door. Strange how the parlor seemed to have dimmed without her in it. Strange how quickly she'd become a part of this house, this family. Strange how she made him feel.

He would miss her when she returned to her comfortable life in Chicago. He would miss her much more than he should.

JENNIFER MADE up her mind in the wee hours of the night. She would write to her father and ask him to send money so that Mick could hire a nurse. As soon as she could find someone to replace her—someone she could trust to take care of Annie, someone who would love her niece as well as see to her physical needs—then she would go back to Chicago. Back to her position at the Angel of Mercy Hospital, back to Mrs. Mulligan's Boarding House, back to Saturday dinners at her father's house, perhaps even back to seeing Harry on Tuesday and Thursday evenings.

Of course, it didn't matter what she went back to in Chicago. She just knew she couldn't stay here. The longer she stayed, the more she would want never to leave. But Mick still mourned the wife he'd lost, and that made staying intolerable.

MICK STARED at the ceiling of the loft. Try as he might, sleep evaded him. He couldn't stop thinking about Jennifer. Sweet, gentle, stubborn, soft, lovely Jennifer.

He desired her, and it surprised him. He wanted her as he hadn't wanted a woman in a long, long time. But what he felt went beyond a physical need. It was something deeper, something much more complex than that, something he'd never felt before.

Maybe this is what love feels like.

Love? No. Impossible. He wouldn't let it be love.

CHAPTER 8

*M*ick?"

He lowered the draft horse's hoof and straightened, looking toward the sound of Jennifer's voice. She moved toward him, wrapped in her woolen cloak, hugging herself for extra warmth. Her cheeks were pink from the cold and her lips—

"May I speak with you a moment?"

Better not to look at her lips. "Sure." He leaned an arm against the horse's broad back.

"It's time Annie had an outing. I'd like to go to the pond where you two used to go skating. Miller's pond, I think she called it. Will you take us there? Perhaps this afternoon."

"The doc said she wasn't to go out in the cold."

"That was weeks ago. She needs to start doing things she likes to do. You can't keep a child shut up in the house all the time. Not even one in a wheelchair."

"I don't know." He shook his head. "Why would you want to take her to the skating pond? She can't skate."

Jennifer stepped close to the corral gate. "Because she was talking about it again this morning. She misses going skating with you. I think it would be good for her to see you on the ice again.

Maybe it would inspire her to try on her skates, too. She's getting better, Mick. Her recovery's going to be slow. She may never be able to do all the things she once could. She'll need lots of encouragement along the way. But she will get better. I'm sure of it."

The certainty and faith in her eyes made him want to kiss her. Not something he should want. "I haven't thanked you for what you've done for Annie. She's been happier since you came. I'm not very good at finding the words to thank you for what you've done. But I do. Thank you, I mean."

"I ... I'm glad I can help," she whispered.

"Me, too." He stepped forward, one stride carrying him to the gate.

The color in her cheeks faded. Her eyes widened a fraction.

"I wasn't too happy when I got your father's letter, saying you were comin' to Idaho." He didn't know why he told her, but he couldn't seem to stop the confession now that he'd started. "I thought Dorothea put you up to it. I was afraid she would try to use you to take Annie back to Chicago." His voice deepened. "I won't ever let her do that."

"Of course not." Her voice was so soft he almost couldn't hear her. "You're her father. She belongs with you." She smiled, the expression bittersweet. "But I shall miss her terribly when I return home."

He hadn't wanted her to come. Then he'd wanted her to leave as soon as possible. But now ...

"When will that be, Jennifer?"

SHE COULDN'T SEEM to draw a breath. He stood so close to her, only the wooden gate between them. She could see his breath in the cold air. She could see the fine lines at the corners of his eyes and the stubble on his jaw.

I don't ever want to leave. If I thought you could love me as you still

love Christina—

"But you'll stay until Annie is well. Won't you?"

She forced out an answer around the lump in her throat. "I ... I'll stay as long as I'm needed." *Or until my father sends enough money for you to hire another nurse.*

"You really think this outing would be good for her?"

"Yes, I do."

"All right. If the sun stays out, we'll go."

She reached forward, placing her hand over his forearm. "Thank you, Mick."

ANNIE'S FACE glowed with excitement as the sleigh whisked across the white terrain. The air was alive with the merry sound of bells, keeping time with the snow-muffled hoof beats of the two horses.

Glancing at his daughter, Mick knew Jennifer was right about this. Annie did need to get out of the house and do more. She'd been shut up far too long.

"Look, Pa!" She pointed toward a fenced pasture where a mare and her woolly-coated colt cantered through the snow. The foal dropped his head, nearly touching his nose to the ground, kicking up his heels. Then he raced away from his mother, running as far as he could before spinning around and hurrying back to her side. "Aren't they pretty, Aunt Jennifer? That's the Miller's place. I got to see Brian's colt the same day he was born."

"Who's Brian?"

"He's my friend. He used to sit behind me in school."

"He doesn't go to school anymore?"

"Of course he does." Annie gave her aunt a puzzled look. "He's only a year older than me."

"Then he'll still be sitting behind you when you go back to school."

The girl's face lit up again. "You're right. He will."

Jennifer had been right about more than this outing. She'd been right to accuse him of mollycoddling his daughter. He'd treated Annie as if she were helpless, and that hadn't been good for either of them.

His gaze shifted from Annie to Jennifer. Her eyes sparkled with the same gaiety as his daughter's. Her mouth was bowed with a merry smile. When she looked at him, he felt his chest grow warm with unnamed emotions.

Or perhaps they weren't unnamed. Perhaps—

But what good was trying to name them? Jennifer would go back to Chicago when Annie no longer needed her.

Unless ... unless she came to want to stay. Unless he could make her want to stay.

WHILE MICK HELD Annie in his arms, Jennifer lifted the wooden stool out of the back of the sleigh and carried it to the edge of the frozen pond. Then she returned to the sleigh for the blankets they'd brought with them. She was turning around when a snow-ball sailed past her head, missing by inches. "Hey!"

She heard Annie giggle as her father leaned over and packed more snow into a ball. "He won't miss again, Aunt Jennifer," the girl called. "Look out!"

Jennifer ducked in the nick of time, but the sudden movement caused her to stumble. Down to her knees she went.

"Look out!" Annie shouted a second time.

Too late. The wintry missile caught her on the shoulder. Snow splattered onto her face.

She struggled to her feet and tossed the blankets in her arms into the sleigh. "If it's a fight you want, Mr. Gerrard, you've picked the wrong girl. I didn't spend *all* my time reading books in the storeroom." She bent down and grabbed a handful of snow, shaping it with quick, deft movements.

His hoot of laughter was all the challenge she needed. She waited until he bent forward to make another snowball of his own, then let hers fly. It hit him on the top of his head.

Annie's giggles grew louder. "She got you good, Pa."

"So it's two against one, is it?" Mick straightened. The smile he wore was playfully ominous.

Jennifer's heart raced in her chest as he stepped toward her. "Mick ..." She swirled and ran from him. She made a full circle around the wagon and horses, her feet sinking through the crusty surface several times, slowing her escape. She had almost reached Annie before Mick caught up with her. The moment his hands alighted on her shoulders she stopped. Apparently he wasn't ready for that, because he didn't do the same. His forward momentum toppled them both into a high drift.

Jennifer sat up, sputtering as she wiped more snow from her face. Opening her eyes, she saw Mick doing the same. His expression made her laugh, and he soon joined in.

"Oh my," Jennifer said when she could speak again. "I haven't done that in years."

"That's too bad." Mick reached forward and brushed a bit of snow from the tip of her nose. "You look very becoming all covered with snow."

Her pulse hiccupped as he rose to his feet and pulled her up beside him. Their gazes held for what seemed a breathless eternity.

Mick was the first to look away. "Guess I'd better get those blankets for you and Annie. I don't want you two catching colds, now do I?"

"No," Jennifer whispered. "No, you don't."

"I'll build a fire, and then we'll see if we can teach you to skate like an Idaho farm girl."

She didn't need a fire to keep her warm. His gaze had already done that.

CHAPTER 9

a s Mick carried his daughter into her room, she said, "I had a good time today, Pa." She yawned. "Can we go again soon?"

"We'll see, pet." He laid her on the bed. "I had fun, too." Leaning down, he kissed her forehead, at the same time brushing the stray locks of hair off her face.

"I liked … skating again." Her eyes fluttered closed, and she yawned a second time. "Liked it … a lot."

Mick smiled. Annie hadn't actually skated, but she'd worn her skates and he and Jennifer had slid her around the pond, holding her upright between them. He'd been surprised at the amount of strength and control she'd shown. She wasn't anywhere close to being able to skate alone—or even stand alone—but his hope for her full recovery had increased over the course of the afternoon.

Annie rolled onto her side, taking the blankets with her. "Pa?"

"Yeah?"

"I'm glad Aunt Jennifer came to … live with us."

"Me, too, pet." He straightened the blankets, then leaned down to kiss her one more time. "Me, too."

"I hope she stays."

He extinguished the lamp before leaving the room. Outside the bedroom door, he paused, and his gaze found Jennifer.

"I hope she stays."

She sat close to the wood stove, mending one of his shirts, a tiny frown puckering the delicate skin between her eyebrows. A soft green shawl lay over her shoulders. She wore a gown the same color as her eyes, and her hair hung loose down her back. When had she blossomed into such a beautiful woman?

She glanced up. A smile curved the corners of her mouth. "Is Annie asleep?"

It seemed so right for her to be sitting near his fire, asking that question.

He nodded.

She laid aside her mending. "I was afraid she was going to fall asleep at the supper table. It was a big day for her."

"I hope she stays."

"It was a wonderful day for me, too, Mick." Her voice was as soft as a gentle summer rain. "Thank you."

He'd like to see her sitting there every night for the rest of his life, and the realization shook him to the core. He went to the kitchen to pour himself a cup of coffee. His hand shook as he picked up the blue-speckled pot. Not surprising. It wasn't every day he thought such things. Not every day he considered taking himself a wife.

Hot coffee splashed onto his hand, but he hardly noticed the pain.

A wife? Was he out of his mind? There hadn't been one moment of happiness in his marriage to Christina. Not even one. If not for Annie—

"You've scalded yourself, Mick. Let me look at it."

He turned, surprised to find Jennifer standing beside him.

She took hold of his hand, cradling it in her own. "Cold water will help." She led him to the sink and placed his hand beneath the faucet. "Leave it there," she said as she pumped the handle.

He could smell her orange blossom cologne. The fragrance seemed to rise up in a sweet cloud, circling his head, filling his nostrils, fogging his mind, breaking down his defenses.

"Jennifer ..."

HER NAME WAS LITTLE MORE than a dry croak in Mick's throat, yet it sent shivers rippling through her body. She swallowed, apprehensive, before looking up at him. There was no mistaking the desire she saw burning in his eyes.

She held her breath as his strong hands closed around her upper arms. He drew her closer to him, and his head lowered. The touch of his lips upon hers was gentle, yet it started a violent storm in her heart.

In all too short a time, he released her mouth, drawing back far enough that he could gaze into her eyes. *Don't pull away, Mick. Can't you see what I feel for you? Please don't pull away.*

Rising on tiptoe, she became the aggressor, kissing him, willing him to know she loved him, wanting him to know this was where she wanted to be. Forever. She heard the growl deep in his throat. Her heart raced in response. His arms closed around her a second time. The world began to spin, and she gave herself up to a well-spring of new emotions and sensations.

Oh, that he would feel for her what she felt for him. Oh, that he could release Christina's memory and find it in his heart to—

He released her so suddenly she almost fell to the floor. Stumbling backward, she gripped the edge of the sink to regain her balance. When she looked at him, she found him without expression. It was if he'd shared none of the wild emotions she'd felt. Still felt.

"I'm sorry, Jennifer. I shouldn't have done that. Forgive me." He spun around, strode toward the door, and left the house, not even pausing to put on his coat.

"Mick," she whispered.

Silence was her only answer.

MICK WAS SHAKING all over by the time he reached the barn, but it wasn't because of the cold. It was the fire within he felt, not the cold of the winter evening. He shook because he'd acted like a kid of eighteen without enough sense to see trouble when it was right in front of his face.

Perhaps he did love Jennifer. But she'd made it clear from the start that her intentions were to return to Chicago. Did he want another unwilling wife, resenting him for making her live so far from the life she'd had in Chicago? Besides, unlike her stepsister, Jennifer was innocent, untouched, worthy of a man's care. He'd come close to stepping over the bounds of what was right. And if he wasn't careful, he might yet do so—and then she would grow to hate him. The way Christina had hated him.

He sank onto a bale of hay and cradled his head in his hands. The truth was, he already felt the pain of missing her. He would miss hearing her cheerful greeting in the morning. He would miss looking at her across the supper table each evening. He would miss seeing the way her pale hair fell over her shoulders, and he would miss the sparkle in her eyes.

He straightened as his gaze turned toward the closed barn door.

He had never felt this way about Christina. How could he, once he'd learned the truth, once he'd learned Annie was the daughter of another man? But perhaps, if he'd tried harder, they could have found a measure of happiness together.

And now? Shouldn't he try harder with Jennifer? If he loved her, wasn't it worth the risk to try? If he'd given up at the first sign of trouble when it came to farming, he'd be back stocking shelves in a mercantile somewhere.

For some crazy reason, he thought of that golden angel in the mail order catalog. Annie had thought Jennifer looked like the angel, and he'd begun to think so, too. He'd begun to hope again. Hope for their future, his and Annie's.

And why shouldn't he hope? Christmas was a season of love. It was a time of miracles. Maybe, just maybe, this was *his* season of love.

IT WAS LATE by the time Jennifer heard Mick reenter the house. In the darkness of her bedroom, she pictured him crossing the parlor. In her mind, she witnessed him performing all his routine bedtime tasks before he climbed the ladder to the loft.

Sick at heart, she rolled onto her side, turning her back toward the door. She closed her eyes and tried to will herself to sleep, but it wouldn't come. Instead, the memory of his kisses replayed in her mind, time and time again.

He'd kissed her, but in the end, he'd rejected her. He'd set her aside, unwanted. Nothing could be more clear. And why had she thought he would want her? She was such a pale, plain thing compared to her fiery, beautiful stepsister.

I must leave soon. I can't wait for Father to send money for another nurse. Tears dampened her pillow. *I must go soon or I'll make an even greater fool of myself.*

CHAPTER 10

*J*ust as Jennifer walked out of her bedroom early the next morning, Mick stepped down from the last rung of the ladder. As he turned around, their eyes met. For a moment, neither of them spoke, neither of them moved. She felt her emotions rising to the surface. Afraid he would read her thoughts, she dropped her gaze to the floor.

"Jen," he said softly, stepping toward her.

She raised a hand to stop him. "Please, Mick. Let's not say anything about last night. I … I'd rather not talk about it." She swallowed, trying to remember the words she'd rehearsed throughout the sleepless night. "I … I know how you feel about Christina, and I also know that I don't belong on this farm. It would be best for me to leave as soon as possible." Her voice fell to a hoarse whisper. "Best for everyone."

"Why?"

Was he being intentionally cruel? Wasn't his rejection of her enough reason? What other one could she give him? She couldn't tell him it was because she loved him and would die if she had to be around him without hope he would ever feel the same. She had some pride left, and she meant to hold its tattered remains around her as best she could.

"There's a man in Chicago who I've been seeing for some time now. Harry. Harry Reynolds is his name, and—" She looked up, and her words died in her throat.

His face was like granite, his eyes as cold as Lake Michigan. "Of course. I understand. If that's what you want, I'll arrange for your passage as soon as possible, but I'd ask you not to go until after Christmas. Annie's counting on you being here. I'm sure your Mr. Reynolds can survive without you that long."

She felt close to tears. "I'd like to spend Christmas with ... with her, too."

"Good." He turned away. "I'd better see to my chores." He crossed to the door, stopping to put on his coat. Then he looked back at her over his shoulder. "I'd just as soon we don't tell Annie that you're leaving. No point in spoiling the holiday for her."

Jennifer couldn't speak around the lump in her throat, so she nodded in reply.

After the door closed behind him, she moved toward the black iron stove. By rote, she prepared the coffee, then set the skillet on the stove and began to cook breakfast.

What had she expected him to do? Beg her to stay? Plead with her to change her mind? Why would he? He didn't love her. He didn't even desire her. She was nothing to him besides his daughter's nurse.

And she wouldn't even be that for much longer.

THIS WAS what Mick got for letting himself believe he was in love. He'd been better off when he'd accepted things as they were, not hoping for something he'd never had. He and Annie had done fine without a woman in their home. They would do fine again once Jennifer was gone.

"There's a man ... Harry Reynolds ..."

Why had he been surprised? He'd heard similar words from Christina. Only he'd never loved his wife. But Jennifer ...

"There's a man ..."

Perhaps she was like Christina after all. Faithless. Devious. And he'd thought he was in love with her. Better he'd learned the truth now than later. He hadn't been as lucky with Christina. Their marriage had been a sham from beginning to end.

If only Jennifer had been different.

If only she could have loved him.

If only ...

~

ANNIE COULDN'T UNDERSTAND what went wrong. Yesterday they'd laughed and had so much fun, but this morning both her father and Aunt Jennifer wore dark expressions. Neither of them spoke a single word after sitting at the breakfast table.

Why did they both look so unhappy? Pa liked Aunt Jennifer a lot. He'd been happier since she'd come to stay with them than Annie could remember him ever being. And Aunt Jennifer was in love with her pa. She knew it as sure as she knew her own name.

Something else she knew. Aunt Jennifer was gonna leave unless Annie found a way to stop her.

An unpleasant memory wrapped around her young heart. Her ma packing a valise. Her parents' voices raised in anger. Annie hiding beneath the covers of her bed, not wanting to hear the ugly things they said to each other. The darkness that enshrouded their home after her ma got in the wagon and drove off. She didn't know how many days or weeks passed between that day and the one when Pa said her ma wouldn't be returning, that she'd died in some far-off place of the fever. It had seemed like years.

She didn't ever want to see her pa that unhappy again. She had

to do something to keep her aunt from going away. Her pa needed
Aunt Jennifer, and Annie needed her, too.

~

IT WASN'T OFTEN a farmer wished he had more things to do, but
that was what Mick wished at that moment. Anything to be away
from Jennifer. Anything to escape the pain nesting in his chest.

Only there weren't any chores left for him to do. He'd already
fed the animals and milked the cow. Since Jennifer's arrival, he'd
repaired everything he could find that needed fixing, both in the
barn and in the house. With a foot of snow on the ground and icy
winds blowing in from the northwest, he didn't have to worry
about plowing or planting or irrigating his fields.

"Pa?"

He looked at his daughter.

"What about a Christmas tree? Shouldn't we have gone to cut
one down before now?"

"We're not going to the mountains this year, pet. The ride
would be too hard on you."

"But we can't have Christmas without a tree, Pa. It wouldn't
seem—"

"Don't worry. Mr. Miller's bringing down a wagon full of pines
for all the folks who can't get up to cut their own. He said he'd
give us first pick. We'll go over to his place tomorrow."

After a moment's consideration, Annie seemed satisfied with
his answer. Her smile returned as she glanced toward the opposite
end of the table. "Will you help me string popcorn for the tree this
afternoon, Aunt Jennifer?"

"Of course. I'd like that."

The note of sadness in Jennifer's voice drew Mick's unwilling
gaze. The same emotion was mirrored in her eyes. He wished he
could believe it was real, but he couldn't. When he found himself
wanting to reach out and comfort her, he hardened his heart.

After all, she was the one who wanted to leave. She was the one who'd kissed him with such abandon, only to tell him she was being courted by another man.

"You'll go with Pa to help him pick out the right tree, won't you, Aunt Jennifer?" Annie's voice dropped to a whisper. "I'm not finished makin' my Christmas presents so I need to stay home."

"Well, I ..." Jennifer glanced up, her gaze meeting Mick's.

"Tell her, Pa. Tell her she has to go with you."

"If she doesn't want—"

"Oh, please, Pa. She *has* to go with you." His daughter's eyes pleaded more eloquently than her words, and he was helpless against them.

He returned his gaze to Jennifer. "It seems your expertise is required. We'll go for the tree tomorrow around noon."

"I'll be ready."

Mick rose from his chair, needing to get away from Jennifer, needing to get out of her sight. Call him a fool, but he still wanted to kiss her every time he looked at her. He still wanted to hold her. He still wanted something he couldn't have.

Her love.

THE SOUND of the closing door made Jennifer flinch.

"You're going away, aren't you?" Annie asked in a whisper. "You're going back to Chicago."

Jennifer turned toward her niece, uncertain how to answer. She'd promised Mick she wouldn't say anything to Annie until after Christmas.

"That's why Pa's sad. 'Cause he doesn't want you to go."

Oh, how she wished that were true.

"My ma left us, too."

Jennifer resisted a welling up of tears. "It's not the same, Annie. Your mother couldn't help leaving you."

"Yes, she could. She didn't have to leave in that wagon with that man. She wanted to go. She told Pa she hated him and she wasn't ever comin' back." She stared at her hands, folded in her lap. "I was glad she wasn't comin' back. She didn't like Pa or me. But you like us. You love us."

"Annie, I don't understand." Jennifer shook her head, trying to make sense of the child's words.

The girl pushed her wheelchair away from the table. "We thought you were going to stay." She rolled her chair across the parlor, disappearing into her bedroom.

Jennifer stared after Annie, a score of unanswered questions racing around inside her head. Christina had left in a wagon? Annie hadn't wanted her mother to come back? Mick thought Jennifer would stay?

"But you love us."

Yes. Yes, she did love them. She loved them both.

A GENTLE SNOW had begun to fall the next afternoon by the time Mick drove the team and sleigh up to the front of the house. He pulled his coat collar up around his neck before he hopped down from the wagon seat. Moments later, the front door opened, and Jennifer stepped into view. A smile curved her mouth as she took in the wintry scene. The simple expression of joy caused his heart to skip a beat.

So lovely. So genuinely giving and caring with his daughter. And so beautiful. White fur trimmed the dark blue hat, framing her face and making her eyes seem even larger than usual. Her warm, woolen cloak was buttoned tight against the coldness of the day, yet Mick had no trouble discerning the gentle, feminine curves that he'd already assigned to memory.

He held out his hand. "Here. Let me help you into the sleigh."

Her smile faded. "Thank you." She placed her fingers in the palm of his hand, her gaze dropping to the ground.

He wanted to recall the anger he'd felt yesterday. He wanted to remember all the bitterness he'd harbored toward the Whitmore family and all the good reasons he'd felt that way. But he couldn't summon the feelings. All that was left was a lonely ache where he'd begun to feel love.

And despite everything, he knew only Jennifer could fill that lonely, empty place inside him.

THE TEAM TROTTED along the country road, the snowfall growing heavier, the temperature dropping. Jennifer huddled within the warmth of her cloak, wondering if it was the winter weather that made her feel so cold or Mick's tense silence.

You're making a mistake. Don't leave. Tell him you're not going away. Tell him that Harry means nothing to you.

She glanced at Mick, who sat stiffly beside her, his jaw set, his intense blue eyes staring straight ahead.

But I can't tell him. Annie must be wrong. He doesn't want me to stay.

But what if Annie wasn't wrong? What if Mick did care about her enough to want her to remain with them? What if there was a chance, no matter how remote, that he might return her feelings, that he might learn to love her, too?

There were so many things she needed to ask, so many things she wanted to know, but she was afraid to speak, afraid to learn the answers. And so they rode on in silence.

SITTING on the edge of her bed, Annie massaged her legs, then straightened them, one at a time, like Aunt Jennifer had taught her to do. It hurt, but she wasn't going to let that stop her. The best Christmas present she could give her pa was showing him she was getting better.

Jesus, make me strong, please. Make Aunt Jennifer want to stay. Make Pa happy again. Please, please, please.

If she could just stand, maybe take a few steps, then surely she could do anything else she set her mind to. Including find a way to keep her aunt in Idaho.

Annie pressed her lips together as she scooted forward until her feet touched the floor. Her heart raced, and dizziness swept over her. "I can do it," she whispered. "I can."

Pushing up with her hands, she raised herself off the bed. Her knees wobbled, and for a second she thought she would topple to the floor. But she didn't. A grin burst across her face. She was standing!

CHAPTER 11

*T*he tree filled a corner of the parlor, its fragrant limbs spreading the pine scent throughout the small farmhouse. Jennifer watched as Mick turned the tree first one way, then the other, until Annie pronounced it just right.

"Here, Aunt Jennifer." The girl held out a box of ornaments. "Help Pa trim the tree." Annie smiled as Jennifer took the box from her hands.

Despite her earlier gloom, Jennifer found herself returning the child's smile. It was Christmas Eve, after all. For now she was with the two people she loved most in the world. There would be plenty of time to be sad after she returned to Chicago.

Following Annie's precise directions, Jennifer arranged the gingham bows and hand-painted pine cones on the tree. Occasionally she would look up and find Mick watching her. Her heart would catch, and she'd hope he would say something, anything. But he didn't speak. There was only silence between them—the silence of two people afraid to take a chance on love.

She turned away from the Christmas tree and crossed to the window. Pushing aside the curtain, she stared out at the snowy blanket that covered the earth. The clouds had blown over, revealing a sliver of moon in a star-studded sky. Silvery crystals glittered on tree limbs and from the eaves of the barn and house. The night sky seemed more blue than black. A beautiful Christmas Eve.

"It's time you were in bed, young lady," Mick said. "Saint Nick won't come until you're fast asleep. Come on. I'll carry you to your room."

Jennifer turned away from the window.

"You don't need to carry me, Pa. You need to stay here and talk with Aunt Jennifer." There was a challenge in her tone.

Her father looked toward Jennifer.

Annie continued, "You've always said it doesn't do any good to keep things that are botherin' me all to myself." She rolled her chair toward her room. "And you always said it never hurts to try. Seems to me you ought to try, Pa. Seems to me you both should try."

Jennifer wanted to look away from Mick, but she couldn't. She wanted to run away before he rejected her again and her heart shattered.

"She's pretty smart for bein' only ten." Mick stepped away from the tree. "We do need to talk, Jennifer."

"We do?"

He loomed tall before her. "We do."

Her heart quickened.

"I've made more than my fair share of mistakes in life, Jen, but if I let you go away without telling you how I feel, that would be the biggest mistake of all." His fingers closed around her upper arms. "The words don't come easy." He pulled her toward him.

Jennifer tilted her head back, scarcely able to draw breath.

"Don't go, Jen. Annie and I want you to stay. We need you." His head lowered, and his lips claimed hers.

It would be so easy to say yes to this man. It would be so easy to stay with him just because he and his daughter needed her. But she wanted more. She wanted his love, and he hadn't offered her that. She pulled free from his embrace, stepping away from him until her back was pressed against the wall. "I ... I can't stay. Feeling the way I do, it would be too difficult for me to live here as your sister-in-law and Annie's nurse." She felt the color flare in her cheeks. "I couldn't live like that."

Mick's eyes widened. Then, after several long moments, he cupped her chin with his fingers. "You don't understand, Jennifer. I don't need you as a sister-in-law. I'm asking you to be my wife."

"Your wife?" An odd rushing sound filled her ears. Somehow, she found herself back in his embrace.

"I love you." He kissed her forehead, then pressed his cheek against her temple, whispering, "I've never said those words to a woman before. I love you, Jennifer. Stay and be my wife. Stay and be Annie's mother. We need you, but we love you even more."

FEAR MADE the blood run cold in Mick's veins. He'd taken the greatest risk of his life to speak those words aloud. Would it be worth it?

"You *love* me?" Jennifer whispered as she shook her head. "But you still love Christina."

He saw it then, the love in her eyes. His fear evaporated like a mist.

"We can talk about Christina later." He cradled her face between his hands. "It's you I love, Jennifer Whitmore. Tell me now. Is there a chance you could love me?"

She waited several heartbeats, then answered, "Don't you know, Mick? I've always loved you. All these years, I've loved you."

When he kissed her again, it was with an overwhelming tenderness. It was a kiss filled with hope for the future. Their future. His and Jennifer's and Annie's.

"Tell me you're never leaving," he whispered when the kiss ended.

This time, she didn't hesitate. "No, Mick, I'm not ever leaving. I'll be with you forever."

~

UNNOTICED, Annie stood on wobbly legs, holding onto the door for support. She watched as her pa and aunt moved across the room to stand beside the Christmas tree. Their arms were wrapped around each other, and Aunt Jennifer's head leaned against Pa's chest.

She heard him chuckle. "I think you and I are more surprised about this than Annie's going to be."

"Mmmm." Her aunt nodded.

"But it's a nice Christmas present, all the same."

Aunt Jennifer lifted her head and looked up at him. "The angel didn't come."

"What?"

"The Christmas angel for the tree. Annie had her heart set on it. I ordered it the day you took me to town, but it didn't come. She'll be disappointed."

Smiling to herself, Annie eased herself onto her wheelchair. Her surprise could wait until morning. For now she was content.

She remembered the night she'd closed her eyes and wished for the Christmas angel. She remembered hoping an angel would look out for her and pa. Not a doll to top a tree. A real one. And that was just what happened, too. The Christmas angel had arrived, and her pa was holding her in his arms right now.

Smiling, Annie closed her bedroom door without a sound.

A CLOUD MOUNTAIN
CHRISTMAS

CHAPTER 1

2007

*M*addie Scott's heart stopped in mid-beat:

SUPER BOWL MVP CRAIG HOUSTON WEDS
ACTRESS SHARI WARD. COUPLE'S FIRST CHILD
EXPECTED IN FEBRUARY.

"Miss? Are you ready?"

She looked toward the convenience store clerk, trying to ignore the humming in her ears.

The girl frowned. "Are you ready to pay for those things?"

"Yes." Maddie grabbed the magazine and dropped it, a bag of chips, and a soda onto the counter. "I'm ready."

The clerk looked at the magazine cover. "That guy's a hottie, huh?"

Please be quiet. Biting her tongue, Maddie pulled a twenty-dollar bill from her wallet and held it toward the girl, hoping that would hurry her along.

It worked. Two minutes later, Maddie pushed through the

glass swinging door of the convenience store and hurried toward her rental car. She unlocked the driver side door of the black SUV with the remote, longing to get inside, away from anyone's view. As soon as the car door was open, she tossed her purchases onto the passenger seat, then slid behind the wheel.

It shouldn't matter. It *didn't* matter. Craig Houston hadn't been a part of her life for over four years. Their five-year marriage had crumbled beneath the weight of his bad habits and extramarital affairs. Her love for him was killed slowly but surely long before the signatures were dry on the divorce papers that had ended both her marriage and her dreams for the future.

"I don't want kids, Maddie. I'm not cut out to be a dad."

Tears pooled in her eyes as the memory echoed in her mind.

The truth was, Craig hadn't wanted kids *with her*. He looked happy enough on the cover of that magazine with his pregnant bride.

She wiped away the tears with the back of her hand. Silly to get upset over this. It wasn't as if she didn't *know* Craig and that actress were an item. She'd have to be a nun in a French Alps monastery to be unaware. Their faces had been plastered in various magazines, week after week, the handsome NFL jock and the gorgeous Hollywood star.

It was the injustice of it all that stuck in Maddie's craw. Here she was, four years after the divorce, swimming in a sea of debt— the debt Craig left her, no less—and her ex-husband was living the high life.

She drew a deep breath. "God, don't let me give in to self-pity. I know that what Craig does and who he marries has nothing to do with me. Help me to quit looking back. Help me to trust You with my future." She turned the key in the ignition and backed the SUV out of its parking place.

By force of will, Maddie turned her thoughts to the reason for her trip into the snowy Idaho mountains. If she did her job, the resulting commission could wipe out her debt. Wouldn't that make this her best Christmas in years?

The two-lane highway wove its way through the foothills, climbing steadily into the majestic mountains. Frequent switchbacks and blind corners kept her speed from topping forty miles per hour, and the white snowscape made her eyes tired, despite her sunglasses. After nine years in Southern California, she was more used to sand and surf than this winter wonderland.

Today was Maddie's first time on this particular stretch of road. Although she grew up in Idaho and had skied on occasion, her idea of the perfect winter holiday was a comfortable chair near a blazing fire, a mug of hot tea in one hand and a good book in the other. Cloud Mountain, her destination, had a year-round population of about six hundred and fifty. Decades ago, it had been a popular ski area, but today it was mostly forgotten, overshadowed as it was by its more famous Idaho cousins such as Sun Valley, McCall, and Tamarack.

Why would anyone invest money in a lodge that—according to all reports—had fallen into serious disrepair, a lodge located on a mountain most skiers didn't know existed? Without a wealthy conglomerate behind them, who could hope to compete against the better-known resorts? She had to wonder about Anthony Anderson, the new owner of Cloud Mountain Lodge. Was he reckless or simply not bright?

Well, at least she was getting a long weekend out of the trip. And tucked away in the mountains of Idaho, she needn't worry about running into Craig and his new bride on the streets of LA.

TONY ANDERSON TOOK several steps backward and stared at the Christmas tree in the corner of the lobby. Colored lights twinkled, reflecting off tinsel, garland, and ornaments. Empty boxes, wrapped like gifts, peeked from beneath the lower limbs of the fragrant pine tree.

"What do you think, Audrey?"

"It's a work of art. Prettiest I've seen in this place in years."

"Good enough to make the guests feel festive for the holidays anyway." He glanced at his watch. "Speaking of guests, is the room ready for Mr. Fairchild's representative?"

"It's ready. Got the new sheets and comforter on the bed and fresh towels in the bathroom. Don't you worry. She'll get the royal treatment while she's here."

"I can always count on you."

Tony thanked the Lord frequently for Audrey Tremaine. The woman was a godsend, no doubt about it. She had worked at the lodge for forty-two years, starting as a maid when she was twenty-years-old. Although she now wore the title of head house-keeper, she did more than keep the place clean and tidy. She pretty much ran it, from manning the front desk to ordering supplies to hiring part time help to making their guests feel at home.

Of course, until they had more guests, he supposed it wasn't all that hard for Audrey to manage the lodge. But if the manuscript brought the price some thought it would, he wouldn't have to worry about money. The renovations of Cloud Mountain Lodge wouldn't take years to complete. He wouldn't have to do the majority of the work himself. The lodge could be bigger and better than his original plans. He had plenty of ideas. What he lacked to make them come true was cold hard cash.

"How about the rooms for the Sullivan family reunion?" He picked up the empty boxes that had held the Christmas deco-rations.

"We're on schedule. All you need is to get that paper hung in the green room."

"I was planning to do that later today." He headed down the hall toward the back door.

Audrey called after him, "Hurry back. Cookie made cornbread and a pot of chili for lunch. It's ready when you are."

"Sounds good. Be right back."

Cold air bit him the instant he stepped outside. He hunched his shoulders as he strode down the steps and along the shoveled walkway to the shed. After tossing the empty boxes inside, he glanced toward the new metal building that housed a workshop, his Jeep, and the used-but-new-to-him snowcat.

All things considered, a great deal had been accomplished since last May when he took possession of the lodge. It felt good, watching it come together. Every day he thanked God for allowing him to live his dream.

He turned and strode back to the lodge, thankful for the warmth that greeted him.

"How was the drive, Miss Scott?" he heard Audrey say. "Were the roads clear?"

A woman replied, "Yes, they were dry almost the whole way. Thank goodness. I haven't driven in snow for too many years."

Sounded like David Fairchild's representative had arrived.

Tony drew a deep breath while checking to make certain the tails of his flannel shirt were tucked into the waistband of his Levi's. "Your will be done, Lord," he whispered, then walked toward the lobby, pausing when he reached the doorway.

Audrey stood behind the counter while the woman signed the check-in form. Three designer bags—well-worn but high quality —and a black leather briefcase sat on the hardwood floor near their guest's feet. She wore straight-legged jeans, snow boots, and a white, down-filled parka. The coat looked new, not surprising since the woman was from LA.

Audrey handed a key card to the guest. As she did so, she saw Tony and smiled. "Here he is now. Miss Scott, this is Mr. Anderson, the man who found the manuscript."

Before the woman turned completely around, before Tony saw more than a glimpse of her profile, he recognized her. Maddie

Scott. Her straight black hair was longer. She looked a little thinner. But it was Maddie.

She wouldn't recognize him, of course. Why should she? He'd been just another guy in college, occasionally hanging around the edges of her life. No competition for the football star who'd captured her heart.

"Hello, Mr. Anderson." She took a step toward him, her hand extended, a warm smile in her voice. "I'm Maddie Scott. Mr. Fairchild sends his apologies for not being able to be here. His plans changed abruptly, and rather than postpone the meeting, she sent me to represent his interests."

Tony took hold of her hand, wondering if it was good news or bad that David Fairchild hadn't come in person. "Welcome to Cloud Mountain, Ms. Scott. It's nice to have you here." That part he didn't have to wonder about. It was nice to see Maddie again, even if she didn't remember him.

"Thank you." She glanced around the lobby. "Looks like you're ready for Christmas."

"Pretty much. Next year we'll do more." *Especially if this deal comes together the way I hope it will.*

A frown furrowed her brow as she looked up at him. "I'm sorry, Mr. Anderson, but do I know you?"

That gave his ego a lift. Maybe he wasn't completely forgettable. "Call me Tony. Everybody does."

She continued to stare.

"We met in college."

"At Boise State?"

He nodded.

"Tony Anderson," she said softly, shaking her head. Then her eyes lit with recognition as she pointed at him. "Anthony Anderson. History of Western Civilization. You used to hang around with Brad Taylor."

Tony nodded again.

"You look different. Didn't you wear glasses?"

"That was me."

"Contacts?"

"Laser surgery." He stepped to her bags, stuck one beneath his left arm, the briefcase beneath his right, and grabbed the other two suitcases by their handgrips. "I'll show you to your room."

They climbed the curved staircase.

"So, are you from here, Tony?"

"No. I grew up on a farm near Twin Falls. But my aunt and uncle had a cabin up here for many years. My folks and I came up a lot when I was a kid. Went fishing and rode horses in the summer, went skiing and snowmobiling in the winter. I always liked it when we got to come to the lodge for supper. That was a big occasion. I loved the rustic look of the place, and the food was good, too." He glanced over his shoulder. "It was already in decline back then, but I was a kid. To me, it was cool."

They arrived at the blue room.

"This is where you'll stay. I hope you find it to your liking."

"I'm sure I will." She slid the electronic key card into the slot and removed it. The green light flashed, and she pushed open the door. "Oh, this is lovely." She walked across the room to gaze out the window.

"Call the desk if you need anything." Tony set her bags inside the door. "Did Audrey tell you we were about to sit down to lunch? Our chef's made homemade chili and cornbread. We'd like for you to join us if you're ready to eat."

"Thanks." She turned toward him. "I'd like that. I am hungry."

That's when he noticed the difference in her, something he hadn't seen earlier. There was sadness in her wide brown eyes, a deep kind of sadness that made his heart ache. And he knew who'd put it there: Craig Houston.

CHAPTER 2

*M*addie sat on the bed and flipped open her mobile phone. Surprisingly, she had service. She hadn't been sure she would in these mountains. She pressed the number for David's speed dial and waited for him to pick up.

"Fairchild."

"Hi, David. It's me."

"Maddie. Are you at the lodge already?"

"Yes. I got in a short while ago. I'm in my room and am about to go down for lunch."

"Have you met Mr. Anderson? What's your take on him?"

She rose and walked to the window again. The view was breathtaking. "Yes, we met. In fact, it turns out I know him. Sort of."

"What?"

"We went to college together. I don't remember much about him. We didn't move in the same circles."

The Tony Anderson she remembered was more of a math geek, a rather shy kid with shaggy hair, a slender build, and glasses, the sort who spent most Friday nights at the library instead of on dates. But that didn't describe the guy who'd escorted her up from the lobby a short while before. This Tony Anderson was confident and rugged with a great smile and the most striking blue eyes she'd ever seen.

David cleared his throat. "Is this going to help us or hurt us?"

She shook her head, more to shake off the image in her mind than in answer to David's question. "I don't think it will make a difference, one way or the other. Don't worry. I'll close this deal before the weekend is over."

"I'm sure you will. You always do."

She hoped he was right. She owed David Fairchild, big time. He and his wife had been her good friends long before David became her employer. In some ways, he was the father she never knew.

Maddie turned to face her room again, staring at the four-poster bed, complete with blue and white canopy. "David, I saw the magazine cover with Craig and Shari on it."

There was a lengthy pause on the other end of the line. "I'm sorry you heard about it that way. I didn't know myself until this morning or I'd have warned you."

"It's okay." She released a sigh. "I was a little surprised about the baby on the way. How'd they manage to keep that out of the news for so long?"

"I don't know. But I do know this. The guy's an idiot. I've met Miss Ward. She's all flash and no substance. Craig's going to be miserable in no time."

"Thanks, David." She smiled sadly. "I'm sure it's wrong of me to like that you said so, but I like it anyway."

He chuckled.

"I'd better go. I've got work to do."

"Well, don't forget to have a good time while you're there. You're in danger of becoming a workaholic. You're young. Live a little."

They said goodbye, and Maddie closed the cover of her phone. Her gaze shifted to her briefcase, but the growling of her stomach intruded on thoughts of work. She hadn't eaten any of the chips she bought at the convenience store. Now her hunger returned with a vengeance.

She hoped the chili and cornbread were good.

~

"SHE'S A PRETTY THING." Audrey took plates and bowls from the sideboard and carried them to one of the smaller round tables. "How well did you know her?"

That was one of the negatives about living in a small town—everybody thought your business was theirs. But Tony didn't try to avoid the question. No point. She would worm it out of him eventually. "Not as well as I wanted to."

"Carrying a torch, huh?"

"No." The word felt like a lie, but it wasn't. Oh, he'd thought about Maddie through the years. How could he help it with her photos, along with Craig's, in magazines and newspapers, especially during football season.

Then came her divorce.

He felt sorry for her. It had to be rough, having your troubles become fodder for a gossip-hungry world. Tony had made more than his share of mistakes, but thankfully, only a handful of people knew about them. When he asked forgiveness or made amends for something, at least the press didn't take pictures and talk-show hosts didn't make jokes.

"Come in, Miss Scott," Audrey said, intruding on Tony's thoughts. "You're right on time."

He turned to watch Maddie enter the dining room.

Ker-thump.

The sensation in his chest was oddly familiar. Familiar because it had happened often around Maddie during his college years. Odd because he hadn't felt it in eight or nine years.

Audrey motioned toward the table. "We serve our meals family style, although Tony's planning for the day when we can operate a full-fledged restaurant again."

He pulled out a chair for Maddie. "Here you go." He felt like a tongue-tied teenager, and that wasn't good. He had business to do with this woman. Important business.

Ker-thump.

Just as Maddie sat at the table, the door to the kitchen swung open, and Cookie entered the dining room, carrying a serving bowl filled with chili and a platter of cornbread.

Cookie's real name was Jacob Smitherman, although few people knew it. In his youth, he was a logger, but an accident left him with a bad leg. That's when he turned to cooking, first for loggers in the camps, later—having perfected his craft—in restaurants around the Northwest. A desire to retire in the central Idaho mountains had brought him to the lodge, for which Tony was more than a little grateful.

Audrey introduced their guest as Cookie set the bowl of chili on the table.

"Glad to have you with us," the older man said to Maddie. "I hear you're from Los Angeles."

"I am now, but I grew up in Idaho."

"Do tell." Cookie took a seat at the table.

With everyone settled, Tony looked toward Maddie. "I like to say grace before we eat when it's just the staff. Do you mind?"

She shook her head.

Tony closed his eyes. "Lord, we thank You for this food and for the hands that prepared it. Bless it to the nourishment of our bodies so that we might do the work You've called us to do. Amen." When he looked up, he found Maddie watching him again, this time with the slightest of smiles bowing her mouth.

Ker-thump.

~

MADDIE COULDN'T REMEMBER the last time she sat down to eat with a group of strangers who said grace over their food. Of course, she usually dined alone or on the go, and her own prayers were often forgotten in her haste.

"So tell us, Miss Scott." The chef held the serving bowl toward her. "Why on earth did you leave Idaho to live in California?"

She scooped chili into a large ceramic bowl. "My husband's job took us there."

"You're married?" Audrey looked as surprised as she sounded. "And here I was, calling you Miss Scott. I'm sorry."

Maddie shook her head. "I should have said *ex*-husband. I'm divorced. Scott was my maiden name, so I guess that makes me *Ms*. Scott."

"How very sad about your marriage. Divorce is a hard thing to go through."

She realized then that Audrey Tremaine didn't know who her ex-husband was. Didn't know who *she* was. It was nice not to be recognized, nice not to have people whispering behind her back. *Isn't that Maddie Scott? Tsk, tsk. Couldn't keep her husband from cheating. What's wrong with her, do you suppose?*

She drew a quick breath, trying to ignore the welling hurt and frustration. She hated feeling this way. It wasn't even about Craig anymore. It was the sense of failure and inadequacy that ate at her.

As if sensing Maddie's turmoil, Audrey changed the subject. "Tony, why don't you tell Ms. Scott how you found the manuscript?"

"She probably knows the story from Mr. Fairchild."

"No, not really. Please tell me." Maddie would listen to him read the telephone book if it would prevent another bout of self-pity.

Tony smiled as he spread honey-butter on a square of corn-bread. "Well, if you're sure it won't bore you."

"I'm sure."

"I'll give you the short version." He motioned with his knife toward Audrey and Cookie. "These two are sick of hearing about it."

The housekeeper protested but not the cook. He rolled his eyes, then leaned over his bowl of chili and spooned some into his mouth.

Tony seemed not to notice. "I'd worked on the lodge about a month when I got to the room at the end of the hall on the second floor of the east wing. The former owners said nobody'd stayed in it since Small's death back in the late fifties. He made this lodge his home for more than twenty years."

Maddie knew a little about the reclusive writer. His most famous works were published in the late 1920s, but there'd been demand for his new efforts—which were few and far between—in the latter years of his life.

"The rumors that he died from foul play kept guests out of that room. Some said he haunts the room where he was murdered."

"I don't believe in ghosts." Maddie squared her shoulders. Did Tony think he would get more for the manuscript if there was something spooky about where it was found? If so, she was surprised. It didn't fit with a man who said thanks to God for his food. Still, she was nobody's fool. She would be careful.

Tony grinned, as if reading her thoughts. "Neither do I. Besides, the research I've done proves Small died of natural causes. It seems his publisher started those rumors of foul play in order to generate sales of his previously published books."

"Oh." She relaxed a little.

"Anyway, like I said, Small lived in that room until his death. Three of the walls had built-in bookshelves and there was a built-in desk beneath one of the two windows in the room. It was when I started tearing things out that I found the manuscript. The pages were tied with string, like a present. About five hundred pages or so—" He used his hands to indicate the thickness of the manuscript. "—all yellowed and scribbled on with notes, changes, doodles. He'd scrawled his name across the first page, too."

"Tony almost threw out the whole bunch," the housekeeper interjected. "He thought it was junk."

He nodded. "Came pretty close to it. I'm thankful Audrey suggested I have somebody look at it before I did."

"And now he has a number of people interested in buying it." Audrey reached over and patted the back of Tony's hand.

Was this lady for real? Or were the two of them working her, hoping to up the price David would pay?

Maddie dropped her gaze to her bowl, wondering when she'd become a cynic. Whenever it was, she didn't like it much.

CHAPTER 3

ony watched as Maddie dabbed the corners of her mouth with the cloth napkin, then placed it on the table beside her empty bowl.

"That was delicious, Cookie." She slid the chair back from the table and stood.

The chef accepted the compliment with a brief nod.

Maddie looked at Tony. "If you'll excuse me, I need to get unpacked. What time should we meet to go over Mr. Fairchild's offer?"

So that's how it was? Down to business, just like that. Although he shouldn't expect otherwise. It was why Maddie came to Cloud Mountain Lodge. Still, Tony wanted to delay the start of the negotiations. Maybe because he feared talking business would bring about her departure too soon. Or maybe because he wanted to make her smile again, a smile that reached into her big brown eyes, the way he remembered her in college.

He placed his napkin on the table. "You're going to be here for four days. There's plenty of time for us to meet. How about we do it in the morning? This afternoon I need to run into town for supplies, and then I've got to hang wallpaper. We've got more guests coming in over the weekend."

"Well ..."

"You had a long drive up from Boise. Kick back and relax a bit. That's what a place like Cloud Mountain is all about. Relaxing. Enjoying the beauty around us."

"I suppose you're right. Morning it is then."

Audrey began to gather the dirty dishes to carry into the kitchen. "There's a lovely fire in the fireplace in the reading room. It's right off the lobby. Once you've got things settled in your room, come on down and enjoy the view. I'll fix you a cup of coffee, if you'd like."

"She prefers hot tea with milk," Tony said.

Maddie looked at him. "How did you know that?"

"I heard you say so."

"When?"

He shrugged, making light of the memory. "I was part of the study group that met in the Student Union Building. I guess I overheard you tell the waitress." He rose from the chair. "I'd better pick up those supplies or I'll never finish that room on time."

He strode from the dining room, mentally calling himself several kinds of a fool. Maddie Scott had been in his lodge barely more than an hour, and already he was acting like an idiot.

Tony grabbed his coat and hat and headed out the backdoor. The slap of cold air was welcome relief.

"Anderson, you've got more important things to think about than her."

Only, what were they?

MADDIE TOOK HER TIME UNPACKING, hanging clothes in the closet, placing other things in the bureau drawers. Her personal care items—favorite brand of shampoo, face cleanser, lotions, makeup

—went in the bathroom. As she turned her attention to the materials in her briefcase, she remembered David's admonition: *"Well, don't forget to have a good time while you're there. You're in danger of becoming a workaholic. You're young. Live a little."*

A sigh escaped her lips. David was right. All she did was work. She had no social life to speak of. Even her involvement at church was minimal. When someone asked her to go to brunch after Sunday service or to come to a women's Bible study or small group meeting, her reply was, "I'm sorry. I have work to do. Maybe next time?"

But next time never came because she was busy then, too.

Maddie sank onto the bed. "Why am I like this?"

Because you're afraid to live.

It was true. She was afraid. Afraid of failing ... again. Afraid of never being free of the past. Afraid that she wouldn't climb out of debt. Afraid to trust others. Afraid to trust herself.

Even afraid to trust God.

It hurt to confess her lack of trust, even silently. She knew it shouldn't be that way. She knew God loved her and cared about her present and her future. But still she was afraid to let down her guard, to embrace her life as it was, as it was yet to be.

As she'd done several times since her arrival, she walked to the large window and looked at the beautiful winter scenery beyond the glass. So different from Los Angeles. She should listen to David. She should take the time to enjoy herself while she was here. Maybe get into the Christmas spirit.

Christmas.

As a child, she'd loved this season—the lights, the hidden presents, the trees, the parties—but now she dreaded it. The month of December was filled with bad memories. Broken promises. Ugly arguments. Shattered expectations. And like icing on a cruel cake, her divorce had become final in December.

She hadn't been in the Christmas spirit since. Her world had been reduced to work, work, and more work.

"I don't want to be like that any longer, God. Help me, please."

~

TONY WAS LOADING the last of the supplies into the back of the Jeep when he saw Maddie coming down the sidewalk on the opposite side of the street, gazing at the window displays of the small shops that lined Cloud Mountain's main thoroughfare. She stopped outside the Candy Corner.

Her white knit cap was pulled low over her ears, and her hands were shoved into the pockets of her down coat. Even from across the street he could tell she was shivering, her shoulders hunched forward. Years in California must have thinned her blood.

He closed the back of the Jeep and headed across the street. When he stepped onto the curb, he asked, "Got a sweet tooth?"

She gasped as she whirled around. "Tony. You scared me half to death."

"Sorry." He grinned. "Didn't mean to."

"You don't look sorry." After a moment, she smiled, too.

"The caramel apples topped with nuts are my favorite. What about you?"

"Almond Toffee."

"Come on." He jerked his head. "My treat."

"Oh, I shouldn't." She touched her hips. "Too many calories."

"A little won't hurt you. Besides you're so thin right now, a good gust of wind could blow you away."

"I don't know ..."

He chuckled as he took her arm and steered her into the shop. The air inside was thick with wonderful, sweet smells.

"I've gained a pound already," she said.

Evie Barrett, the owner of the Candy Corner, came out of the kitchen, wiping her hands on her apron as she approached them on the opposite side of the candy displays. "Hey, Tony. How you doin'?"

"Good, Evie." He motioned toward Maddie. "This is Maddie Scott. She's a guest at the lodge for the weekend."

"Nice to meet you, Maddie. This your first time to Cloud Mountain?"

"Yes."

"Have you been skiing yet?"

"No. I only arrived at the lodge a short while ago."

"Well, you'll see what I mean when you do. I was up there with my sons yesterday after they got out of school. Great powder this week." She patted her fingertips on the display case. "What can I do you for?"

Tony answered, "We'll take a pound of the almond toffee and a half dozen of the caramel apples with nuts."

"Comin' right up."

Maddie looked at Tony as if he'd lost his mind. "A pound?"

He shrugged.

"I'm in so much trouble," she said beneath her breath.

He laughed.

She smiled in return.

If he could capture that moment and keep it in a jar, he would. It was perfect. The two of them, like old friends, smiling and laughing in a candy shop. It was his best dream come true.

Except in his best dream, they would be more than friends.

Slow down, Anderson.

He turned to watch Evie weigh the almond toffee on the scales.

He hadn't really *known* Maddie in college. He'd *wanted* to know her. So had plenty of other guys. But she never had eyes for anyone but Craig Houston. All Tony could do back then was stand on the sidelines and wish he were more like the football star.

Maybe things could be different now. After all, God wasn't

surprised when Maddie showed up at the lodge. Maybe this was part of His plan.

Or it could be my wishful thinking.

Either way, it wouldn't hurt to find out which it was.

Tony paid for the candy, then motioned toward one of the small white tables that stood along the opposite wall. "Let's indulge."

"Okay. I shouldn't, but okay."

After they were seated, Tony handed her the small white bag of toffee. She reached inside and withdrew a piece. As she bit into it, she released a moan of pure pleasure.

"That good, huh?"

She nodded. "That good." She popped the rest of the piece into her mouth.

"I suppose I shouldn't ask questions while you're eating."

"No. Go ahead. Save me from myself."

He leaned back in the chair. "I was wondering if you've still got family in Idaho."

"No." She shook her head. "My dad died when I was a toddler, and Mom never remarried. When my sister, Kate, moved to Florida with her husband, Mom moved there too. I was still with Craig at the time—" A shadow passed over her face. "—and we were never home much. So it made sense for Mom to live near Kate." She took another piece of toffee from the bag. "What about you? What have you been doing since college?"

"I got my degree in business management and put it to use with a conglomerate down in Texas. I did well, but I missed Idaho. So when I heard the lodge was on the market, I started planning and saving. A few years later, I took the plunge."

"Is your family still in Twin Falls?"

"No. Mom and Dad both passed away while I was in Texas."

"I'm sorry. Was it an accident? They must have been rather young."

Tony twirled the stick on a caramel apple between his thumb

and index finger. "Cancer took Mom six years ago. Dad had a heart attack a few months later."

"I'm sorry," she said again.

"Even after six years, there are still times when something happens and I think, wait until Mom and Dad hear about this." He shook his head slowly. "I guess you never completely get over losing your parents."

Silence stretched between them, each lost in thought. For Tony, those thoughts were good ones, pleasant memories of his parents when they were healthy and happy. He missed them, but at least he had the assurance of the Scriptures that he would see them again in heaven.

Finally, Maddie said, "I'm assuming there's no Mrs. Tony Anderson."

"Not yet." He grinned. "But hopefully some day."

"Do you have some special girl in mind?"

How about you, Maddie?

It was crazy, how close he came to saying those words aloud. It was insane that he thought them at all. Maybe he'd better end this conversation before he made a complete fool of himself. He needed to get away from Maddie and breathe in some crisp winter air to clear his head so he could think straight again.

But when he opened his mouth, he said something unexpected. "Listen, why don't I skip hanging wallpaper and you skip the rest of your window shopping in beautiful, downtown Cloud Mountain? Let's go skiing instead." He leaned toward her. "Let me show you why I wanted to move here and buy that old lodge."

She shook her head. "Tony, I haven't skied in years. I'm not sure I remember how. Besides, I don't have any gear."

"We can take care of all that. Besides, skiing is like riding a bike. You don't forget. We'll take a nice easy run. No steep trails. No moguls."

"I don't know."

"Come on. The sun is shining. The sky is clear. The snow is good. You'll have fun."

"Fun," she echoed softly, lowering her gaze to the bag of candy on the table. "Have some fun." When she looked up again, resolve filled her gaze. "Okay. Let's do it."

CHAPTER 4

*T*ony Anderson was a liar. Skiing was nothing like riding a bike.

Terror tightened Maddie's throat as the lift carried them higher up the mountainside.

Why did she agree to do this? She was never comfortable on skis, never much good at it. Hadn't she sprained something or other back in high school? She was much better at cheering others on from the warmth and safety of the lodge. Only the truly adventurous wanted to rocket down the side of a mountain on two toothpicks.

"Relax, Maddie."

She glanced at Tony. "Is it that obvious?"

"Afraid so."

"What happens when we get to the top? I don't remember how to get off this thing."

He pointed to where the lift deposited skiers before turning sharply for its return to the bottom of the mountain. "Just let your skis carry you off the seat and down the ramp. I'll be right beside you. You did fine down below. This isn't much different."

He was wrong about that. There was a great deal of difference between staying upright on the bunny slope and staying upright while plunging down the mountain she could see below.

Why did I listen to David? This isn't fun!

"Ready, Maddie? Here we go."

Was he kidding?

Somehow she found her skis flat against the ground and her bottom rising off the chairlift. Next thing she knew, she was down the ramp and stopped out of the way of the skiers who'd disembarked behind her.

"Good job." Tony grinned as he lowered his ski goggles into place. "Told you it wouldn't be hard."

She tried to return his smile, but it was a half-hearted effort.

God, get me down this mountain in one piece. Please.

Tony pointed with one of his poles. "That's the easiest trail on the front side of the mountain. I'll lead the way and set a nice, slow pace until you're comfortable."

I won't be comfortable until I'm back in the lodge.

"Ready?"

She nodded. "As ready as I'll ever be."

He pushed off in front of her, his skis gliding over the snow without a sound. Drawing a quick breath, she followed suit, albeit without the same fluidity of motion. It was obvious, even to Maddie's untrained eyes, that few skiers used this particular trail. Probably too tame, even for the kiddie set. Which meant it might be okay for her.

Hmm. This wasn't too bad. She was managing to keep her skis parallel. Her knees were nicely flexed. No problem with the poles.

Lean. Turn. Glide.

Lean. Turn. Glide.

No, this wasn't bad at all.

Tall, snow-covered pine trees rose on either side of the track. Sunlight filtered through their branches, casting lace-like shadows across the snow in front of her. Despite the frigid air,

Maddie felt warm inside her snow-pants, down-filled parka, knit cap, and insulated gloves.

She might actually get to like this.

In front of her, Tony skied back and forth across the width of the trail. About every third turn, he glanced back in her direction, no doubt to see if she'd fallen yet. This time when he looked back, she gave him a thumbs up, letting him know she was A-OK.

Or not.

The almost level trail changed without warning. She felt the downward pull of the mountain. Her skis responded, moving faster over the snow. Maddie's heart quickened right along with the skis.

Too fast ... too fast ... too fast.

If Tony looked at her again, Maddie was too busy to notice. She needed her skis to behave.

Snow plow ... snow plow ... snow—

"Maddie!"

Her name on Tony's lips was the last thing that made sense to her. Then the world turned upside down and inside out. Her right ski went this way and her left ski went that way. She hit the ground—snow wasn't nearly as soft as it looked—and felt it scrape her cheek before she tumbled, head over heels, for what seemed an eternity. She came to an abrupt halt at the base of an innocent looking fir.

"Maddie?" Tony knelt beside her.

She looked up at him, dazed.

"Don't move yet. Let's make sure you're all in one piece."

Don't move. Was he kidding? With everything spinning like a top? She didn't want to ever move again.

"How many fingers am I holding up?"

She groaned. This wouldn't have happened if David Fairchild hadn't told her to have fun. Better a workaholic than lying on her back in the snow while—

"Maddie? How many fingers?"

"Three. You're holding up three." This was too embarrassing for words. "I'm all right, Tony. The only thing hurt is my ego." She placed her elbows on the ground and pushed herself into a sitting position at the exact same moment her brain registered the pain shooting upward from her right leg. It stole her breath away. She dropped back to the ground.

"You're not all right."

Eyes closed, she clenched her teeth. "No."

"Where does it hurt?"

"My right leg. My ankle, I think. I don't know. I'm not sure. It hurts everywhere."

"We'll need a stretcher to get you down the mountain." He was silent a few moments. "I'll have to leave you alone while I get the Ski Patrol. There's nobody else in sight. Will you be okay?"

"Yes." She wondered if she sounded as uncertain as she felt.

"Let's get my coat around you. We don't want you taking a chill while I'm gone."

Maddie feared she might start to cry, and the last thing she wanted to do was blubber like a baby in front of someone she had to negotiate with in the next few days.

"Here you go. I'll lift you up enough to slide the coat under your back. Ready? Here goes."

Tony's voice was quiet, but somehow it was strong, too. Her fears lessened.

"Can you open your eyes?" he asked. "I need you to look at me."

She complied.

"Now keep your eyes open. You need to stay alert. If someone comes down that trail, ask them to wait with you until I get back. I won't be long. I promise." He squeezed her hand, emphasizing his words.

"I'll be okay. Stop worrying and go."

He gave her a nod, his eyes filled with concern, and then he was gone, *swooshing* his way out of sight. The silence of the snowy mountain fell around her. She shivered, wishing she hadn't sent him away so soon.

It already seemed a long while since he left.

~

IF THIS WAS A DOWNHILL RACE, Tony might have given Bode Miller a run for his money. But no matter how fast he went, it wasn't fast enough. He remembered too well Maddie's pale face as she told him she would be okay. She hadn't looked okay. Pain had been evident in her big brown eyes.

Why hadn't he listened to her when she said she wasn't a good skier? Why hadn't he been content to buy her a treat in the candy shop?

Simple. Because he'd wanted to spend time with her. He'd wanted to enjoy her company before they got down to the business of negotiating over the Uriah Small manuscript. Four days was all she would be here, and he'd wanted to make the most of those four days. Skiing seemed the natural option. It was, after all, why people came to Cloud Mountain, to ski and enjoy the great outdoors.

But Maddie hadn't seemed all that excited about joining him on the slopes. She'd been hesitant from the start. He'd talked her into it for selfish reasons. Her accident was his fault.

"Idiot."

As soon as he reached the base of the mountain, Tony contacted the volunteer Ski Patrol. Next he asked the lift operator to call Dr. Martin and make sure he was waiting for them at the clinic. Then Tony got back on the chair lift, anxious to reach Maddie, hating the thought of her lying there alone in the snow, cold and scared.

Relief overwhelmed him when he turned a bend in the trail and saw two other skiers waiting with Maddie. As he drew closer, he recognized them. Gary and Betina Patterson. The brother and sister, both in their early twenties, had moved to Cloud Mountain this past summer to manage the local hardware store for their great-grandfather, Jake Patterson.

Gary saw Tony and came to meet him. "She told us you'd be here any minute."

"How's she doing?"

"In pain but trying not to show it."

"The patrol should be right behind me." He skied forward. "I'm back, Maddie. We'll have you down the hill soon." He knelt across from Betina. "I know you're hurting. I'm sure sorry it happened. I shouldn't have brought you up on the lift. You were doing fine down below."

She gave him a game smile. "It isn't your fault. I could have declined your invitation."

"Right now, I wish you had."

She winced. "Right now, so do I."

Tony glanced over his shoulder, willing the Ski Patrol to hurry up.

IN HONOR of the Christmas season, Maddie opted for a red moon boot on her broken ankle. If she had to be miserable, she might as well be festively fashionable too.

"No weight on that leg for two weeks," Dr. Martin told her as he dried his hands. "Use the crutches. Fortunately, the break is in the distal fibula and doesn't involve the ankle joint itself. You should be able to get around without crutches in a couple of weeks."

"I'm supposed to drive back to Boise on Monday."

"Sorry, young lady. No driving for now."

"But—"

"No driving." The doctor shook his head. "Not for at least two weeks."

Wasn't that just terrific? How was she supposed to get back to LA if she couldn't drive? It wasn't like Cloud Mountain had an airport where she could catch a flight. Two weeks? What would she do with herself for two weeks? Her negotiations with Tony wouldn't take but a couple more days. And then what? Besides, she couldn't afford to be away from the office for that long. There was no way she could stay here for two weeks. She would have to hire someone to drive her to Boise.

"How long will I be in this boot?"

"Six to eight weeks."

Perfect. Just perfect.

"Don't worry about where you'll stay," Tony offered. "We'll move you to one of the rooms on the ground floor. It isn't as nice as the one you're in now, but you'll be comfortable there. Audrey and I will make sure you don't need for anything."

Maddie cringed on the inside. How could she be a tough negotiator if Tony thought her needy and helpless? There must be something else she should say, something else she should do. She pressed a hand against her forehead, trying to focus her thoughts. If she could think straight—

"Take another one of these pain pills when you get back to the lodge." The doctor spoke to Maddie, but he handed the prescription bottle to Tony. "They'll make you sleepy, but that's a good thing. It'll keep you down and your leg elevated."

But I'm not supposed to be sleeping. I'm supposed to be working.

"I'll send in a wheelchair to see you out to your car."

Maddie hadn't the energy to do anything else but nod.

CHAPTER 5

*T*he pain in her ankle, combined with the narcotics Dr. Martin prescribed, caused time to pass in a blur. Whenever Maddie awoke from her drug-induced sleep, Audrey Tremaine was somewhere nearby, waiting to attend to her needs.

In one of her more lucid moments, Maddie called David to tell him what had happened to her. "But don't worry," she added at the end of her tale. "I'll wrap up this deal in a few days."

"I'm not worried about that. I'm worried about you. Are you sure you're getting proper care?" His voice sounded fuzzy and distant. "Is there anything you need?"

"Mmm."

"Maddie?"

Darkness threatened at the edge of consciousness, then spun inward, narrowing the light until it was a mere pinprick. "I need to go now." Without saying goodbye, she closed the cell phone and left it on the pillow as she drifted into a place of strange dreams.

TONY STARED at the screen on his office computer. He was supposed to be attending to bookkeeping chores, but his thoughts were down the hall in the unfinished guest room where Maddie lay sleeping. That's pretty much all she'd done in the two days since the accident.

With a groan, he leaned back in his chair and stared at the ceiling. "This is a fine mess."

Maddie came to the lodge to negotiate the purchase of the manuscript. If Tony—his old college crush reawakened—hadn't been so het up about spending time with her, she wouldn't be lying in that room with a broken ankle and he might already have a sizable check to deposit into his dwindling checking account. If only he'd kept his head out of the clouds and his thoughts on business.

But Maddie always did have a crazy affect on him. The way he'd felt about her back in college never made sense. They probably hadn't exchanged more than a few dozen words in those years at BSU. And yet he'd fallen for her. Hard. He'd looked forward to every study group where she might participate. He'd listened to everything she had to say. Sure, he'd known he didn't have a chance to win her attention. She was Craig Houston's girl from the start, and there was never any doubt about that.

"I must be nuts." That was the only explanation for the old feelings stirring back to life the moment Maddie walked into this lodge.

He rose from the chair and left his office, glancing toward the front desk as it came into view. Audrey was nowhere in sight. Maybe she was in with the patient. Quick strides carried him down the hall to the guestroom. He hesitated a moment, then rapped on the door.

Maddie answered, "Yes?"

"It's Tony. May I come in?"

There was a brief silence, then, "Yes."

He turned the knob and opened the door.

She was sitting up in bed, her back propped with pillows. Two more pillows were tucked beneath her right leg. She wore a pink sweatshirt and a pair of black warm-up pants with the right pant leg cut off at the knee. Her ebony hair was caught in a ponytail on the top of her head. Although her face seemed pale, he thought there was less pain in her eyes.

"How're you feeling?" He stepped into the room, stopping near the threshold, his hand resting on the doorknob.

"Better, I think."

"You look better."

She smoothed her hair. "I'll bet."

"No, you do. Really."

"Well, if I do, it's because Audrey has taken such good care of me."

"She loves to mother people."

"She's been very kind. But I feel like such a bother." She looked at the bottle of narcotics on top of the nightstand. "I don't think I'll take any more of those pain pills. At least not during the day. They really knock me for a loop. I can't stay awake, let alone think straight."

"You probably needed to sleep. How's the pain?"

"Bearable."

"Is there anything I can get for you?"

"No. I have everything I need. But would I be in anyone's way if I moved to the reading room for a while? It might be more pleasant to work out there than in here."

He let his gaze move over the guestroom—the dark paneled walls, the worn forest green carpet, the single window that faced the storage shed. "Sorry about the dismal accommodations. It seemed better to have you on the ground floor."

"I didn't mean to sound like I was complaining about the room. Please don't apologize." She blushed as she lowered her eyes. "It would be awful if Audrey had to climb the stairs to wait on me."

She looked up again. "In fact, that should stop. I know she has other things to do."

Tony thought that extra color in her cheeks was most becoming. She looked lovely. Sweet. Vulnerable. Kissable.

Ker-thump.

Kissable?

Easy there, Anderson. He decided now would be a good time to leave.

Clearing his throat, he pointed at the crutches leaning against the wall near the head of the bed. "Can you manage those all right?"

"Yes, I can manage."

"Okay then. I'll leave you in peace." He gave an abrupt nod and slipped out of the room.

Kissable, indeed.

Ker-thump.

⟿

THE MOMENT THE DOOR CLOSED, Maddie covered her face with her hands. Did she look as flushed as she felt? Oh, she hoped not. School girls blushed, not career-focused businesswomen.

But she feared the worst. Her skin was warm to the touch. And why? Because, right in the middle of telling Tony she wanted to work in the reading room, she'd noticed how ruggedly handsome he looked in that plaid flannel shirt, blue jeans, and work boots. And then she'd thought how small the room felt with him standing in it. Small and ... intimate.

Oh, my. Those pain pills had done more than make her sleepy. They'd made her lose all commonsense.

Moving with care, she lowered her legs over the side of the bed, grimacing as the throbbing in her broken ankle intensified. But it was bearable, as she'd told Tony.

Tony ... Could he possibly be the same guy she remembered

from college? Glasses. Kind of skinny and very quiet. Smart but shy. Maybe her memory was flawed. Maybe she was thinking of someone else.

Which, of course, didn't matter in the least. It wasn't some college kid who wanted to sell a collectable manuscript to David. It was a businessman who needed cash flow.

"Back to business, Maddie," she whispered as she reached for the crutches.

It took longer than she anticipated to wash up in the bathroom. There wasn't much she could do with her hair except leave it in a ponytail. However, she wasn't leaving this room without mascara and lipstick. She didn't want to frighten the guests who were supposed to arrive today.

She chose a dark brown sweater from the clothes in the dresser, but she didn't change out of the warm up pants. She wasn't willing to cut off a leg from any of the trousers and jeans she'd brought with her from California. Not unless she was forced to.

Ready at last, she slipped the strap of her computer case over her shoulder and, leaning on the crutches, made her way out of the guest room, down the hall, and into the lobby.

Audrey Tremaine was behind the front desk, speaking to someone on the telephone. Her eyes widened when she saw Maddie.

Maddie released the grip on her right crutch and motioned with her hand, indicating she didn't need help. Then she continued across the lobby. In the reading room, a fire crackled on the hearth and the scent of pine garlands filled the air. Christmas lights twinkled around the frames of the windows and across the fireplace mantel. Outside the sky was a crisp and cloudless blue, sunlight making the snow sparkle.

How beautiful! The light from the windows and the warmth of the room were like a caress. She felt ten times better than she had five minutes before.

After a quick perusal of the room, she chose an overstuffed chair near a north facing window. A nearby wall socket would provide electricity for her laptop, and she wouldn't get as much glare on the computer screen as she might have in one of the other chairs.

She set the computer case on a coffee table, then sank onto the chair and laid the crutches on the floor. The throbbing in her right foot reminded her that she needed to elevate it.

As if summoned, Audrey appeared in the doorway. "Goodness gracious. Are you sure you should be moving about this soon?" She bustled into the room.

"I'm sure." Maddie glanced toward the loveseat against the opposite wall. "But I could use a pillow for under my foot. That way I won't worry about scratching the coffee table with this boot."

Audrey fetched two throw pillows from the loveseat and brought them to Maddie. "Here. Let me help you." She moved the computer case to the floor, replacing it with the pillows, then lifted and placed Maddie's right leg atop them. Next she drew a side table away from the wall and positioned it next to Maddie's chair. "How about a nice cup of tea? And don't tell me it'll be too much trouble because it won't."

She smiled. "Tea would be lovely. Thank you."

The moment the housekeeper left the room, Maddie drew a deep breath, letting it out slowly. The throbbing in her ankle had worsened over the past few minutes. No surprise, she supposed. She hadn't been up much since her fall.

She leaned her head against the back of the chair and closed her eyes, drawing another deep breath. There. It wasn't so bad now. She would simply relax for a short while, and then she would be ready to attend to some work.

The assigned ring of her cell phone announced a call from her mother. Oh, no. What would she tell Mom? She could imagine Doris Scott's reaction. Mom would want to fly out to take care of her. She wouldn't care that the break was minor or that Maddie could manage fine on her crutches.

Better not to mention it.

She flipped open the phone. "Hi, Mom."

"Hello, dear. How are you enjoying your visit to Idaho?"

"There's lots of snow." That seemed like something safe to say.

"Have you done anything fun?"

"I'm here on business, Mom. Remember?"

"Oh, I know. But I was hoping that you would have a good time. You never seem to do anything fun for yourself."

She swallowed a sigh, wishing her mother didn't worry about her so much.

As if she'd heard Maddie's thoughts, her mom said, "I want you to be happy, dear. That's all."

"I know. And I love you for it. But I'm okay." *Apart from a broken ankle and some persistent self-pity.* "I love doing what I do."

For the next few minutes, they talked about Kate and Don and their two kids and everyone's plans for Christmas. Then, fearing the spotlight might return to her—and worse, that she might be forced to tell her mom about her broken ankle—Maddie decided it was time to end the call.

"I'd better get back to work, Mom. I'll call you after I return to LA. Give my love to everyone."

"I will, dear. You take care. We love you, too."

Flipping the phone closed, Maddie looked out the window. From here, she could see the main ski lift, seats rocking and swaying as they headed skyward. If she hadn't gotten on that silly thing, she wouldn't have to be afraid to talk to her mother. If she had stayed in the lodge where she belonged, she wouldn't—

Right then, Tony appeared outside the window. He carried an ax against his right shoulder as he walked with long strides toward a large tree stump that poked up from the snow. Once there, he swung the ax downward, cutting into the surface of the stump. A nearby wood pile explained his intent.

Maddie leaned to one side for a better view as Tony set to work, chopping large chunks of wood into fireplace-sized pieces. He swung the ax in a smooth arc, and the air *cracked* as the blade bit into the logs. Then he jerked the ax free and repeated the cycle again. He made the work look easy. He even seemed to enjoy himself.

And she enjoyed watching, too. Just look at him. A man in his element. What woman wouldn't enjoy watching him?

She squeezed her eyes closed, alarmed by her wayward thoughts. The last man she'd enjoyed watching as he worked broke her heart into a million tiny pieces. How many football games had she attended, cheering Craig on? How many interviews had she watched on television, her heart swelling with pride?

And how many promises had he broken? How many lies had he told her? How many women had he bedded?

Not all men cheat on their wives.

No, but some of them did. And if Craig could fool her into thinking he loved her and would cherish her and be faithful to her, why couldn't the next guy fool her too?

She didn't even want a "next guy." One mistake was enough.

Maddie hated being divorced. Everything in her had longed for a lasting, God-centered marriage, to be one-half of a couple who would grow old together. When she pledged herself to Craig, she thought he believed in commitment and fidelity. How could she have *not* known the type of man he was? How could she have been so naïve, so blind to the truth?

Because I chose to be naïve and blind.

She never wanted to make the same mistake again.

"It's been almost four years, Maddie," a friend had said to her a month ago. *"It's time for you to get back in the game."* Her response was what it had always been: *"Not interested."*

She opened her eyes and stared out the window, her gaze alighting on Tony.

Jerk. Swing. *Crack.*

Jerk. Swing. *Crack.*

Heaven help her. She needed to conclude her business and get out of here.

CHAPTER 6

ony was stacking the last of the chopped wood in the rack outside the back door when two SUVs, a minivan, and a Jeep pulled into the lodge parking lot. This had to be the Sullivan family.

He stomped his boots on the mat to make sure he wouldn't track up the clean floors, then opened the door and headed toward the lobby.

"They're here," Audrey announced.

"Yeah, I saw them pull in."

In many ways, the newly-arrived guests—sixteen adults and one toddler—would be a test for Tony and his small staff. The Sullivans, their guests for a full week, would fill the eight rooms in the second story west wing of the lodge. He'd worked like a dog to make sure all was ready for their arrival. The last roll of wallpaper had been hung in the green room late last night.

"I'll go help with the luggage." He glanced at his watch. It was not quite eleven. "Better let Cookie know the Sullivans are here."

"I already did."

"Thanks, Audrey. You're always one step ahead of me."

"Been doing it a long time, that's all."

Tony pulled open the front door and stepped onto the porch. With a wave, he called, "Welcome to Cloud Mountain." Then he descended the steps to meet and greet his guests.

It didn't take long to ascertain that the Sullivan clan was a boisterous bunch. The patriarch was Sam Sullivan, newly-retired from the construction business at the age of sixty-eight. Square-jawed with a Kirk Douglas dimple in his chin, he had a full head of gray hair and looked like he'd pumped iron for most of his life. Karen, his wife, was short and round with a mischievous sparkle in her green eyes. Having three sons probably required a great sense of humor.

The second generation of Sullivan men and their wives all looked to be in their forties. Mike, Roger, and Kip Sullivan took after their father in height, looks, and build.

The five members of the third generation were more diverse. Somewhere between their late teens and mid-twenties, there were three granddaughters—two of them with husbands, one of those with a red-haired child in arms—and two grandsons, one of them married, his college-aged brother single.

When the introductions were finished, the Sullivans emptied the backs of their vehicles of numerous suitcases and tote bags, plus sixteen pairs of skis and boots and three ski boards.

Tony grabbed four suitcases and led the way inside. Something told him the lodge was going to feel much smaller with this family as guests.

MADDIE WAS AWAKENED by a commotion in the lobby—and was none too happy about it. She'd been dreaming something delightful, although she couldn't remember what. It had vanished the instant she awoke. She wished she could bring it back.

Straightening in the chair, she moved her laptop to the coffee table. Her arms felt sluggish, as did her mind.

A burst of raucous laughter caused her to start. Who on earth was making all that racket?

Just then a little girl, perhaps a year or so old, toddled into view. She hesitated when she saw Maddie. Her eyes widened, then she squealed in delight and hurried forward, every unsteady step looking as if it would be the last before she fell.

"Iris," a deep male voice called. "Come back here."

The toddler giggled in response. Obviously she had no intention of answering the summons.

"Iris, you heard me. Listen to Daddy."

A fair-haired man appeared in the doorway at the same moment the child arrived at Maddie's chair and hid her face against Maddie's right thigh.

"I'm sorry," the fellow said. "Iris doesn't meet any strangers. She thinks everyone is a friend."

"It's all right." Maddie ran her hand over the little girl's soft wispy curls.

The young father crossed the room in a few strides, captured Iris around the waist, and whisked her into the air. She squealed and laughed again as her dad pressed his lips into the curve of her neck and shoulder and blew.

Maddie felt a pinch in her heart, a longing so strong it stole her breath away.

If only ...

As if to torture herself, she recalled the tabloid photo—Craig and Shari, joyously awaiting the birth of their child.

If only ...

"Did you do that on the ski slopes?"

Pulled from her unhappy thoughts, she wasn't sure what Iris's dad meant.

He pointed at her propped leg. "Did you break something skiing?"

It was Tony who answered. "Actually, she was fine while skiing. It was the falling that got her into trouble." He grinned at

Maddie as he entered the room. Turning toward the other man, he said, "Your wife's headed up to your room."

"I'd best get a move on then." He nodded at Maddie. "See you around."

"Yes." She waved at the little girl. "Bye, Iris."

The child waved back.

Tony said, "Cute kid."

"Adorable." Sorrow tightened her throat once again, sorrow for the might-have-been wishes and why-not questions.

"Hope she didn't disturb your work."

"I wasn't getting much done anyway." She drew a deep breath, determined to stop thinking about what she couldn't have. There were other things that should be on her mind. Completing her business with Tony Anderson, for one. "You know, we should discuss the matter of the manuscript some time today. I need to leave soon and—"

"You're not supposed to drive with that broken ankle. Remember?"

"Don't worry. I'll work out some way to get home. But in the meantime ..." Realizing that rushing back to Los Angeles didn't sound as good as it should, she let the sentence drift into silence.

"In the meantime, it's down to business," Tony finished for her.

"Yes."

He checked his watch. "How about three o'clock in my office?"

"I'll be ready."

"Okay." He motioned toward the table near her elbow. "Do you need anything? More tea or maybe some hot chocolate."

"Thank you, but I'm fine. I'll wait for lunch."

With a nod, Tony left the room.

Maddie turned her head to look out the window as tears pooled in her eyes and loneliness coiled around her heart. She would close this deal and head home, but no one would be there waiting for her when she got there.

If only ...

Stop it. Stop feeling sorry for yourself.

She had much to be thankful for. God had walked her through each stage of grief that followed the death of her marriage. By His grace, she'd come to understand that, while God hated divorce, He did not hate the divorced. He did not hate her. He loved her. He'd collected her tears in a bottle, as the psalm said, and recorded each one in His book. He knew her sorrows and wanted to heal them completely.

Then why don't you trust Him with your future?

CHAPTER 7

*M*addie's quiet meal with Tony, Audrey, and Cookie on the day she arrived stood in stark contrast to today's lunch.

The Sullivans were a gregarious lot who, like the youngest member of the clan, knew no strangers. They treated Maddie like a long-lost member of the family and included her in their conversations as they passed serving bowls around the table.

"Doug broke his leg skiing," Hannah Sullivan said. "When was that, Doug? Four years ago?"

"Five years, Mom. I was a junior in high school."

His brother, Eric, jabbed Doug in the shoulder. "I'll bet Maddie wasn't doing something stupid the way you were."

"Shut up, bonehead."

"Loser."

"Poser."

Some fraternal shoving ensued.

"I apologize, Maddie," Mike Sullivan, their dad, said. "They've been shut up in the car for too many hours. We need to get them fed and out on the slopes where they can burn up some of that energy."

"They don't bother me."

The truth was, it was more bothersome seeing all the happily married couples seated around the tables. Seeing the way Sam deferred to his wife. Watching the tender exchanges between Iris's parents. Hearing Mike's laughter when Hannah told a joke.

Three generations of happy marriages—and her. She felt like a fifth wheel.

"Are you here alone?" Karen Sullivan asked.

Maddie nodded. "Yes."

"What made you choose Cloud Mountain for a solo vacation?" This question came from Iris's father, Wayne Gruber.

Maddie's head ached. "Actually, it's not a vacation." She rubbed the pressure point between her eyebrows. "I'm here on business." *And if I'd remembered that, I wouldn't have a broken ankle.*

Audrey entered the dining room and walked over to Maddie, leaned down, and whispered into her ear. "There's someone here to see you."

Maddie drew back so she could look the woman in the eyes. "To see *me*?"

Audrey nodded, then turned her head. Maddie followed her gaze to find David Fairchild standing in the dining room entrance.

"David?"

He moved toward her.

"What are you doing here?" She lowered her leg to the floor and, bracing herself on the edge of the table, began to rise.

David's hand on her right shoulder gently pushed her back onto her chair. "I came to see how you're doing. Lois and I were worried. You didn't sound like yourself when you called."

Maddie wanted to crawl into a hole and pull the earth over her. "I'm fine, David. It isn't anything serious."

Wasn't it bad enough that she hadn't yet begun negotiations with Tony? Now her employer had made a special trip from California to make sure she was okay. Or worse. Maybe he didn't trust her to close the deal. What had she said to him over the phone when she was in that drug-induced haze? It must be something awful if it made him fly to Idaho in his corporate jet.

Shoot me now!

"Mr. Fairchild." Tony appeared at her left elbow. "I'm Tony Anderson. Welcome to Cloud Mountain Lodge."

Maddie swallowed a groan as the two men shook hands about twelve inches in front of her face.

"It's a pleasure to meet you, Mr. Anderson."

"The pleasure's mine. Will you join us for lunch?"

"Thank you. I'd appreciate it."

Tony motioned toward the smaller table where he'd been seated a few moments before. "There's an empty spot over here."

David patted Maddie's shoulder. "We'll talk after lunch."

She nodded, forcing herself to smile.

As soon as David moved away, Ann Gruber asked, "Is that your father?"

"No." Oh, that miserable, sinking feeling in the pit of her stomach. "He's my boss."

Tony tried not to be obvious as he sized-up the millionaire. Despite his steel-gray hair, David looked a good ten years younger than his age. Moreover, he had an air of confidence that was not uncommon in men of power and wealth.

Before Tony turned his back on the corporate world, he'd known a number of men much like Fairchild—successful, empire-builders, men with the Midas touch. And some of them were the most miserable human beings a man would ever hope to meet.

Something about David Fairchild said he wasn't miserable. He wore an air of confidence and contentment as easily as Tony wore a pair of Levi's and work boots.

"I hope you're planning to stay with us for a day or two." He passed a bowl of mixed vegetables to David.

"Well, at least overnight. Assuming you have a room available."

"We do."

David glanced toward Maddie. "How is she?"

"Better today. The break isn't bad. The doctor says it should mend without a problem, as long as she takes care not to walk on it too soon."

"I'll make certain of that."

Tony wasn't sure he cared for the proprietary note in David's voice. Was there more to his relationship with Maddie than being her employer? He frowned, not liking the train of his thoughts.

He'd done a fair share of research on David Fairchild after receiving word of his interest in buying the Small manuscript. One thing Tony had learned was that David and his wife, Lois, had been married for thirty-one years. By all reports, it was a good marriage. Others looked up to David Fairchild, speaking of him as a man of integrity, a natural leader, someone with a strong personal faith. He didn't seem the type who would be unfaithful to his wife or who would take advantage of a woman young enough to be his daughter.

"Maddie says she knew you in college."

Drawn from his thoughts, Tony answered, "We didn't know each other well, but yes, we were at BSU at the same time."

"I've tried to talk her into going back to school to finish her degree. She doesn't lack many credits." David shook his head slowly. "It's a shame she married Houston. He wasn't good to her."

"You know Craig?"

"I know him." The dark tone of his voice spoke volumes more than those three simple words.

And Tony liked him for it.

~

MADDIE WAS thankful when the meal ended. She smiled and waved at the Sullivans as they emptied out of the dining room, still talking and laughing as they had throughout the meal. Unless she'd misunderstood, they were all headed for the ski slopes, with the exception of Iris and her great-grandmother Karen who were both going to lie down for a nap. Maddie wouldn't have minded a rest herself, but that wasn't possible now.

She saw Tony rise from the table and bid David a good afternoon. Then he nodded in Maddie's direction before leaving.

"Pleasant fellow." David walked to Maddie's table. "I enjoyed our visit. He said you're meeting with him at three."

"Yes." She drew a quick breath and let it out. "Would you like to join us?"

His eyes narrowed slightly. "No. I believe you'll do better without me."

Maddie hoped the surprise didn't show on her face. She'd been certain he came to the lodge because he thought she would blow the deal. She should have known better. It wasn't David's style.

He sat in the chair next to her. "I've taken a room for the night and will head back tomorrow, unless you need me for something."

"If it weren't for my rental car, I'd plan to go with you. Maybe I could arrange for someone to—"

"No, Maddie. I want you to stay here until the doctor releases you. Enjoy yourself. Remember? Do something fun. Relax. Make a vacation of it."

"Not much fun I can have with this." She motioned toward her foot, propped on the chair to her right.

David stood. "You might be surprised." He grinned. "Now, I imagine you need to prepare for your meeting with Tony, and I'd like to have myself a look around Cloud Mountain. Maybe I'll try out the slopes for myself."

"Don't break anything."

He chuckled. "I promise." With a wave of his hand and a "See you later," he turned and strode out of the dining room.

Maddie shook her head. Could this business trip get any stranger?

CHAPTER 8

$\mathcal{T}$ony had most of the clutter cleared off his desk by the time Maddie rapped on the jamb of his office doorway. "Are you ready for me?"

He stood. "Yes. Please come in." He motioned to a chair in front of his desk. "I've got a stool for you to rest your foot on."

"That was thoughtful. Thank you."

As Maddie maneuvered herself into position with her crutches, Tony rounded the desk and took her briefcase from her, setting it on the floor beside her chair. Then he stepped over to the door and closed it.

"I told Audrey to hold any calls so we won't be interrupted." He returned to his chair and sat down.

"I don't expect this meeting will take long." Maddie opened the file folder she'd taken from her briefcase. "As you know, Mr. Fairchild has verified the authentication of the Uriah Small manuscript. Based upon his research into fair market value, he is prepared to make the following offer." She handed him a piece of paper.

Tony's heart started to race as he looked at the figure. Two hundred thousand dollars. And that was the starting point. He knew enough about negotiating to know one never opened with their top offer.

But even if the offer went no higher, this would allow him to put a new roof on the lodge before next winter. He could update the plumbing in the west wing. And the kitchen. There ought to be enough that they could start remodeling the kitchen. Wait until Cookie heard the news!

Tony leaned back in his chair, hoping his excitement didn't show on his face. "I was wondering. What does Mr. Fairchild intend to do with the manuscript, if it's his?"

"He'll see that it's published. He knows he isn't the only fan of Small's writing and doesn't want to keep it to himself. It should be released so others can enjoy. But the original manuscript will be preserved in his private collection."

"Does he have a large number of collectible manuscripts?"

Maddie's demeanor was all business, her reply measured. "David collects many things. His interests are eclectic. This will be the first manuscript he's acquired."

Tony liked it better when she wasn't so businesslike. "Tell me something. How did you happen to go to work for him?"

"I'm not sure what that has to do with—"

He leaned forward, resting his forearms on the desk. "Humor me."

She watched him in silence, as if trying to figure out what would bring about the best results for her employer.

Tony offered her a slow smile. "I'm curious, Maddie." He could have added, *to know more about you.* That's what he wanted—to know more about Maddie Scott. To know everything about her.

A touch of color painted the apples of her cheeks before she lowered her gaze to the folder on her lap. Perhaps he wasn't as good as he thought at disguising his feelings. Maybe he didn't even want to be good at it.

Talk to me. Tell me about yourself, Maddie.

She looked up, her gaze softened. "David and Lois befriended me not long after we moved to Los Angeles. They could tell I was a fish out of water and took pity on me."

"You? A fish out of water?" That was hard to envision. She'd seemed confident in every gathering during college.

"Very much so."

"How did you meet the Fairchilds?"

"David is a good friend of the team's defensive coach, and our paths crossed at different functions."

"And that's when you went to work for him?"

"No." She shook her head. "I wasn't employed while ... while Craig and I were married. But after the divorce, I—" She broke off suddenly and again lowered her eyes, but not before he caught the glint of pain.

Was she still in love with her ex-husband?

Maddie drew a deep breath and stiffened her shoulders. "The truth is, David's offer of employment was a godsend. Without a degree or an employment history to fall back on, I had little hope of making much of a living. Certainly not enough to help me pay off my debts."

"Debts?"

"I know what you're thinking." She gave him a self-deprecating smile. "Everyone assumes I received a large settlement in the divorce. However, I wasn't very smart. I didn't hire an attorney right away. I was so sure God wouldn't let the divorce go through that I kept procrastinating. I kept thinking Craig would change his mind, and all would be well. Denial with a capital *D*. In the end, I agreed to things I shouldn't have. I let myself be tricked and coerced by Craig and that shark of a lawyer he hired."

"I'm sorry, Maddie. I didn't mean to pry or bring up bad memories."

"You didn't know."

"It was insensitive to ask."

She was silent for a long moment, then said, "You weren't

insensitive, Tony. You've been nothing but kind to me since I arrived."

He'd like to be even more kind, if she'd let him. He'd like to prove that he was the sort of guy who wouldn't hurt her or trick her or coerce her. If she would just give him enough time to prove it.

~

TONY'S GAZE made Maddie go all quivery on the inside. There was something sweet and gentle about it. Something that made her want to stay right here in this chair and bask in it.

Which was the very reason she decided it was time to leave.

She reached for her briefcase. "You think about that offer, Tony, and we'll talk again tomorrow, if that's all right with you." She stood.

"Yes. That's a good idea. We'll talk tomorrow afternoon." He rose from his chair, went to the door, and opened it for her. "Would you like help with your briefcase?"

"No, thanks. I'm getting the hang of these crutches, and the briefcase is light." With scarcely a glance in his direction, she left the office and returned to her guest room.

What happened back there?

She sank onto the side of the bed and replayed the brief meeting in her mind. It hadn't gone at all as she'd expected it to. Usually she got some sense of a person's reaction to the initial offer. Not so with Tony. She hadn't a clue whether he thought it too low or much higher than expected. What was she going to tell David when he asked how the meeting went? She and Tony hadn't said more than a few words about the offer. Certainly nothing that could be called negotiating. And how in the world had they arrived at the topic of her divorce and her resulting debt?

She groaned.

"Maybe I can blame it on those stupid pain pills."

Except she hadn't taken one today.

"Humor me."

She remembered the deep timbre of Tony's voice, the smile that slowly curved the corners of his mouth.

"I'm curious, Maddie."

Her stomach fluttered again, as it had when he'd spoken those words in his office. Not good. Definitely not good. She had a job to do, and it didn't include an attraction to the proprietor of the Cloud Mountain Lodge.

She released a sigh. Nothing about this trip was going as expected. From that lousy tabloid headline to her broken ankle to this less-than-professional start to her negotiations on David's behalf.

Pull yourself together. Now.

Another deep breath. There. She felt better. The next time she met with Tony, she would stay focused on the business at hand.

IT DIDN'T TAKE Tony long to find David Fairchild. The man was sitting in the Grounds for Happiness Coffee Shop at the corner of Main and Third, enjoying a tall drink.

"Mind if I join you?" Tony asked.

"Not at all." David waved to the other chair at the table. "Please do."

Tony caught the eye of Nancy, the barista, and nodded. He'd been in here often enough since buying the lodge for her to know what to bring him. He liked his coffee black and strong.

"So what do you think of our little town?" he asked as he sat opposite David.

"Nice. Some interesting shops, and the people are friendly. I met one elderly gentleman who knew Uriah Small rather well."

"Walter Hopkins?"

"Yes. He was a fount of information about Cloud Mountain in

the mid-Twentieth Century. And about Uriah Small. We had quite a fascinating discussion."

Tony chuckled. "Walt knows a lot about many things. I hope my mind is as sharp when I'm half his age."

"Amen to that." David took a drink from his coffee cup. "Walter also said he hopes the publicity about the manuscript will bring more tourists here to ski."

"The whole town hopes that." Tony removed the lid from the coffee Nancy brought to the table. Steam rose in a translucent ribbon above the cup. "May I ask you something? About Maddie."

David cocked an eyebrow but said nothing.

"She says you and your wife have been good friends of hers for quite a while."

"Yes."

"So you must know her pretty well. Especially since you two work together now."

"Maddie's like a daughter to us."

Tony could see how that would happen. The Maddie he remembered from their college days had drawn people to her with an easy smile and enchanting laugh. More than once he'd observed her helping someone that other students on campus hadn't noticed needed help. Perhaps it was her genuine kindness that had made him want to know her better. She'd been part of the "cool crowd," but it hadn't gone to her head.

If not for Craig Houston …

He blew across the coffee in his cup before taking a sip. "I know she got burned in her marriage. Is she over it?" *Is she over him?*

David frowned. "I'm not sure that's any of—"

"I only ask because I care about her … A lot."

Silence stretched between them. Tony knew he was being sized up and hoped he passed muster.

At long last, David said, "I see."

"In case you're wondering, this doesn't have anything to do with the manuscript."

"Strangely enough, I believe you." The older man nodded. "And because I believe you, I'll answer your question. Yes, she's over Craig. But the hurt is still there. He left some deep scars."

Tony hadn't liked Craig Houston back in college, but he didn't know if that was because the guy was a jock or a jerk. Maybe both. Either way, Craig had taken Maddie's love and thrown it away. That made him the lowest of life forms in Tony's book.

He rose from the chair. "Maybe I can do something about those scars." He snapped the lid onto the coffee cup. "At least I'd like to try."

CHAPTER 9

"Oh good. You're here."

Maddie looked up from the paperback novel to see Hannah Sullivan standing in the entry to the reading room, her granddaughter Iris braced on her hip.

"We've signed up our family to go on a sleigh ride tonight. We'd like you to join us."

Maddie laid the book, open face down, on the coffee table next to her foot. The invitation was tempting. She was growing bored with sitting around. She was used to being more active.

Ann Gruber stepped into view to stand next to her mother. "Please come. The guys will make sure you don't hurt your ankle while we're out."

By "the guys," Maddie assumed Ann meant her husband and two brothers.

"It's a horse-drawn wagon bed on skids with bells, lights, and hay bales," Hannah said. "The driver says the route takes about an hour. He'll pick us up here at the lodge at seven and bring us back by eight or so. Ought to be pretty out with the full moon."

"It does sound like fun, but I may need to meet with David when he returns and—"

"Oh, I'm sorry." Hannah laughed. "I should have told you. We saw Mr. Fairchild in town on our way back to the lodge, and he's planning to go on the sleigh ride, too."

Maddie felt her eyes go wide. "He is?"

"Yes."

"Well then, I'd love to join you." How could she turn down an opportunity to see the distinguished President and CEO of Fairchild Enterprises sitting on a bale of hay? In fact, she'd better take her camera. Lois would want to see some photos of that.

"Here, Mom." Ann held out her arms. "Give me Iris. I need to change her diaper."

Hannah kissed the toddler on the top of her head before passing the child to Ann. "I'll be up shortly." After her daughter and granddaughter left, Hannah entered the room and sat on the loveseat across from Maddie. "It was lovely on the mountain today. The snow is perfect. Most of the family is still at it. I hope the skiing stays like this the whole time we're here."

"How long will that be?"

"Through next Sunday. It's a Sullivan family tradition. Every third year, we meet somewhere to celebrate an early Christmas together, nine days and eight nights, the whole lot of us. Three years ago, we went to Hawaii, but this year we decided we wanted to enjoy a white Christmas. My father-in-law came to Cloud Mountain to ski years and years ago and stayed in this lodge. He didn't even know if it was still open, so he was excited when he found the web site and was able to book us in." Hannah looked around the room. "It's a lovely old place, isn't it?"

"Yes. It has—" Maddie sought for the right word. "—character."

"I agree. Mr. Anderson's done an admirable job of modernizing it without sacrificing any of its charm."

Maddie nodded.

"I can see why he wanted to restore it, and I admire his courage. It isn't easy to leave what seems safe and secure to pursue your dreams."

"No," Maddie answered softly. "It isn't." *I admire him, too. I wish I had some of that same courage.*

From outside came the sound of stomping boots mixed with laughter.

"The crew has returned." Hannah rose from the loveseat. "I'd best go hurry my men along or they'll never be ready for supper. See you there."

Maddie listened as the Sullivans left their skis and boots on the porch, then spilled into the lodge and made their way up the stairs to their rooms. A twinge of envy tightened her chest. She'd often wished to be part of such a family—large, extended, demonstrative. She used to imagine herself with three of four children, going for a visit to her sister in Florida. All the little cousins running and playing. Laughter and love blended together in perfect harmony.

What a beautiful dream that had been.

More voices intruded on her thoughts—David's and Audrey's, coming from the lobby. She reached for her crutches and got up from the chair, but before she had time to move around the coffee table, David appeared in the doorway.

"Did you hear about the sleigh ride?"

"Yes, I heard. I was on my way to my room. I need to decide what to wear." She looked down at her right leg. "This could be a problem."

"It won't be. We'll take along lots of blankets. That'll keep you snug." He crossed the room and draped an arm around her shoulders, giving her a fatherly-type squeeze. "I'm glad you agreed to go, Maddie. It'll be good for you to do something fun."

"It was doing something fun that got my ankle broken." She rolled her eyes at him. "Besides, I couldn't very well refuse the invitation since you're going. Lois will want me to tell her all about it. You'll leave out too many details for her satisfaction."

"Ah, you know me well."

"Yes, I do."

David took a step back. "So how did your meeting go with Tony?"

"I'm not sure." She hated admitting what a poor job she'd done at the outset of the negotiations, but there was no way around it. "We ... we got sidetracked. Completely my fault." She lifted her chin in a show of confidence. "We're going to talk again tomorrow afternoon, and I'll make sure we stay on topic."

Her boss smiled. "I'm not worried. In fact, I don't mind if you give him more time to weigh his options. After all, you won't be leaving on Monday since you can't drive. You can afford to take your talks with Tony a bit slow." He paused a moment and his voice deepened. "I like that young man, Maddie. He has vision and drive. He'll put the money he gets from selling the manuscript to good use. Of course, I want to be the buyer, but even if not, I'll hope for the best for him."

She couldn't have explained why, not even to herself, but she was pleased by David's approval of Tony. "I'll do my best to make sure he accepts your offer."

"I know you will. Never doubted it for a moment." He took another step back. "I'd better let you check on your wardrobe for the sleigh ride. We can talk about the negotiations before I leave tomorrow. But no thoughts about business tonight."

TONY WOULDN'T NORMALLY JOIN his guests on a sleigh ride, but nothing about life at the lodge was normal at present. Not as long as Maddie was among his guests. So when Hannah Sullivan suggested he come along—and he learned that both Maddie and her boss were going—he was quick to agree.

His first priority was to make sure he got to sit beside Maddie before one of Sam Sullivan's single grandsons got there first. Those boys might be eight to ten years younger than Maddie, but he doubted that would stop them from flirting with her. He'd already observed some of that over dinner—and hadn't been any too pleased about it either.

Nick Robertson and his son Randy drove two bobsleighs into the lodge's parking lot a little before seven o'clock. The sleighs weren't fancy—modified wagon beds with runners, each sleigh pulled by a pair of black Percherons—but the Christmas lights strung from front to back made them look like carriages fit for a princess and the bells on the harnesses chimed a merry tune.

"Do you need help out to the sleigh, Maddie?" Doug Sullivan asked.

Before Maddie could answer, Tony said, "He's right. It isn't a good idea for you to try to walk out there in the snow with those crutches." He took the closest crutch from her and gave it to Doug. "You hold this, and I'll carry Maddie." Then he swept her into his arms. She looked at him with wide eyes, and he prayed he hadn't moved too fast for his own good. "Better give Doug that other crutch. It'll make it easier to carry you down the steps."

She complied without looking away.

Man, she had beautiful eyes. Chocolate brown pools that revealed a hint of vulnerability, a touch of wistfulness. And her mouth ... A generous mouth, ripe for kissing.

Ker-thump.

He swallowed hard as he carried her down the porch steps and out to the nearest sleigh. Nick had a stool waiting at the back of the wagon bed, and Tony climbed it, keeping a protective grip on the woman in his arms. With care, he set her on one of the side benches, her back against the outer rail. Then he pulled one of the hay bales close for her to use as a prop for her right leg. All this he accomplished while blocking the way for anyone who might try to sit beside her.

By the time Tony tucked a blanket around Maddie's right leg and took his seat on the bench on her left side, the rest of the group had found their own places in the two sleighs. But he gave little notice to who was where. He only cared that Maddie was by his side.

"Do you go on these sleigh rides often?" she asked, a slight smile bowing the corners of her mouth.

"No, this is a first for me here in Cloud Mountain. The last time I took a sleigh ride it was a junior high church event."

"How about you, David?" Maddie turned her gaze to the other side of the wagon. "How many sleigh rides have you been on?"

Her boss chuckled. "Not many opportunities in Los Angeles."

"What about when you and Lois vacation in Aspen?"

"Not yet. Maybe next time we're there." He was quiet a moment, then said, "On second thought, maybe we'll skip Aspen and come to Cloud Mountain. Lois would like it here."

Nick climbed onto the driver's seat and took the reins in hand before tossing over his shoulder, "Here we go, folks. Hold on." He slapped the leather reins against the horses' rumps, and the sleigh slid into action.

As if on cue, the moon—full and so large it seemed within reach—rose above the western ridge.

"Oh my." Karen Sullivan pointed. "Isn't it beautiful?"

Everyone in their sleigh looked at the moon. Everyone except Tony. He continued to feast his eyes on Maddie, her face brushed with moonlight.

Beautiful.

Silence fell over them as the sleighs left the town behind. The only sound was the soft *shooshing* of the skids sliding over the snow-covered trail.

Maddie turned her head toward Tony. When their gazes met, the smile she wore slowly faded until all that was left was the look of vulnerability he'd glimpsed earlier. The breath caught in his chest. It would be easy to lean forward and capture her lips with his own. Would she welcome his kiss or despise him for it?

From the other sleigh came the sound of voices raised in song.

"Silent night ... Holy night ... All is calm ... All is bright ..."

Soon, those in the sleigh with Tony chimed in.

"Round yon Virgin ... Mother and Child ... Holy infant ... so tender and mild ..."

Maddie's voice was soft but crystal clear. It seemed to wrap around Tony's heart and squeeze it.

Is it crazy to feel the way I do? She's only been here a few days and yet ...

"Sleep in heavenly peace ... Sleep in heavenly peace ..."

And yet I can't stand the thought of her not being here. Lord, is it possible she might want to stay?

ONE CHRISTMAS CAROL led to another and another and another. The music seemed to belong in the forest, rising above the sleighs, swallowed by the stately pine trees and snowy mountainsides. And with each note Maddie sang, her heart grew lighter.

Hope. That's what she felt. Hope.

She cast a surreptitious glance in Tony's direction, not surprised when she found him still watching her. She wished the trees weren't obscuring the moonlight just now. She would like to see what was behind his unswerving gaze.

But perhaps she knew already. She'd seen several emotions in the depths of his eyes earlier—attraction, tenderness, kindness. He seemed a solid sort of man, one whose feelings were steady and sure.

Why do I think that's true about you? I've known you such a short while.

"Don't stop singing," he said softly. "You've got a lovely voice."

"Do I?"

"Yes."

Despite the chill in the night air, her cheeks grew warm, making her thankful for the darkness.

"I was wondering." He leaned closer. "Would you like to go to church with me in the morning?"

He was so close, she felt the warmth of his breath on her cheek, making it hard to focus on his words. What was it he'd asked her? Something about church. Oh, yes. Did she want to go to church with him?

"I think you'd like it there," he added. "It's a small congregation, but the preacher knows how to teach the word and the choir is pretty good too."

She couldn't recall receiving a nicer invitation in years. Maybe not ever. She'd been asked to attend movie premieres and art exhibits, the opera and the ballet. While still married to Craig, she'd been a guest at countless parties in houses the size of some palaces, surrounded by women dripping with diamonds. But nothing sounded as pleasant as going to church with Tony Anderson.

"What do you say?"

She drew a quick breath and answered, "Yes."

His smile widened as he drew back a few inches. "Great." Then, as if it were the most natural thing in the world, he rested his right arm on the rail behind her back.

Maddie's heart thrummed as a pleasant warmth spread through her veins. How easy it would be to lean against him. How nice it would be to trust again.

If only she could.

CHAPTER 10

*F*ortunately for Maddie, she'd packed two business suits, one of which had a skirt. Wearing a skirt to church would mean she didn't have to cut a leg off a pair of her good slacks, something she was loathe to do.

Somehow she managed to bathe and dress on Sunday morning without injuring another part of her anatomy in the process. Then, as satisfied as she could be with her appearance, she hobbled into the dining room just as the Sullivans were finding places at the tables. David was there, too, and when he saw her, he pulled out the chair next to him and motioned for her to be seated.

"How did you rest?" he asked as she drew near.

"Like a rock. All that smog-free night air did me good. I didn't even need a pain pill."

David nodded. "Glad to hear it." He took her crutches and set them against the wall. "You look nice. I understand you're going to church with Tony."

"Yes. Will you join us?"

"Wish I could, but I'd best hit the road after breakfast. I told the pilot I'd be at the airport by eleven."

She straightened on her chair. "But we were going to talk about the negotiations before I meet with Tony again."

"I gave that some thought, and I don't think it's necessary." He took the cloth napkin from beside his plate and spread it open on his lap. "Maddie, you know what to do. You're good at it."

Yes, she knew what to do. She was a competent negotiator in ordinary circumstances. But doing business with Tony didn't feel ordinary.

David leaned closer. "Trust your instincts."

"Easy for you to say."

"I have confidence in you."

She wished she could say the same about herself, but she couldn't. Everything about this trip seemed off-kilter. First there'd been that headline about Craig and Shari and their pregnancy. Then there'd been her broken ankle, something that never would have happened if she'd kept her mind on business. And now? Now there were these ... *feelings* about Tony, feelings that had nothing to do with negotiating the purchase of the Uriah Small manuscript for David's collection, nothing to do with closing the deal so that she could collect her commission and pay off her debts. Feelings she could ill afford to entertain.

Not now.

It wasn't worth the risk.

~

REDEEMER COMMUNITY CHURCH looked like something off a Currier and Ives Christmas card. Wood siding, painted white. Long and narrow with plenty of windows. A tall steeple. Snow piled high all around, the mountains rising majestically behind it. Pine wreaths with red bows decorating each of the double doors at the entrance.

As Maddie climbed the steps, she felt Tony's gentle touch on the small of her back, a gesture of support, a silent message that he wouldn't allow her to fall. Emotion tightened her throat. She didn't want to be so moved by his unspoken concern, but she was.

"Maddie, this is Luke Matthews, our pastor. Luke, I'd like you to meet Maddie Scott."

Tony's words of introduction pulled her attention to the man standing inside the doorway. She smiled as she took the minister's proffered hand.

"Glad you could join us today, Miss Scott."

"Thank you."

The pastor cast his gaze downward at the red boot on her right leg. "Did our mountain do that to you?"

"Yes."

"I hope you'll forgive us." Luke looked dutifully remorseful.

Maddie laughed. "I believe I will."

She and Tony moved through the narthex, stopping several times for Tony to make more introductions. The small sanctuary was exactly as she imagined every country church should looks— scuffed hardwood floor, wooden pews with faded red seat cushions, a choir loft big enough for ten people at most, an upright piano on the right side, a raised pulpit on the left.

Tony stopped beside the third pew from the front and waited until she was settled, her crutches beneath the pew in front of her. Then he sat down beside her.

Softly, she said, "I feel like I've stepped into the church in that old Disney movie, *Pollyanna*. Don't you think so?"

"Sorry. Never saw it." In contrast to the ordinary words of response, his voice was low and intimate. "Not exactly a boy's kind of movie."

She felt heat rise in her cheeks. "No, I suppose not."

"A favorite movie of yours?"

"No, but I've seen it lots of times. My mom owns the DVD. She loves it." Maddie was babbling now but couldn't seem to help herself. "She'd love this church, too."

"How about your church in LA? What's it like?"

"Very different from this one." She looked away, once more allowing her gaze to travel around the room, taking in the stained glass window and the life-sized wooden cross. "Very different."

"Is it a big church?"

"Very large. About ten thousand members."

"Must be many opportunities to serve in a church that size."

Chords from the piano ended their conversation, and Maddie was thankful. Tony's last comment had struck a nerve. Her church did have many places and ways for its members to serve, but over the past few years, Maddie had been less and less active. She blamed it on work and frequent travel. But those were only excuses. True, perhaps, but excuses all the same.

As the congregation stood, Maddie listened to Tony's voice raised in song and knew, deep in her heart, that he wasn't the sort of man to offer excuses. She suspected he was deeply involved in this small church and with the people of his community.

And she envied him.

PASTOR LUKE, preaching a series on the fruit of the Spirit, was in great form today.

Thanks, Lord.

Tony couldn't help it. He'd wanted Maddie to hear a good sermon, one that would show that this church might be small but it embraced truth and the Author of truth.

Is that pride on my part, Father?

Maybe so, but he thought not. Redeemer Community was a boon to everyone in the area, not only to those who attended services here. When there was a need, its members were the first to show up and the last to leave. In the almost eight months he'd lived in Cloud Mountain, he'd seen this church in action, and it was one more reason he knew he'd made the right decision when he moved to Idaho and bought the lodge.

Would any of that be enough to make Maddie want to settle here? And as much as he'd like to deny it—not being the sort of man who fell in love in at first sight—having Maddie stay in Cloud Mountain was what he wanted. He wanted her with him. He wanted to love her and care for her, to laugh with her and cry with her.

I can't explain why I feel the way I do about her, God. Could this be Your doing? You had to know it was Maddie who would come to negotiate for the manuscript. You had to know her being here would stir up all those old memories and lots of new feelings. Is it Your will that she stay? Is it Your will that I love her?

He hoped so. Because as much as he wanted Maddie with him, he wanted God's will more.

Help me to know what Your will is, Father.

THE SULLIVAN CLAN—WITH the exception of Sam, Karen, and Iris —had left for the ski slopes before Maddie and Tony returned to the lodge. It made for a more serene Sunday dinner for those who remained behind. The conversation around the table flowed easily from one topic to another, from construction to the stock market, from the fall movie season to the latest hot novels being touted by the talking heads, from the current snow pack to the advantages of all-wheel drive vehicles.

Maddie enjoyed every moment, but her favorite part was when Sam Sullivan asked Tony to tell them about his decision to leave the corporate world, return to Idaho, and restore this old lodge. She loved seeing the way excitement lit his eyes as he answered the question. There was no mistaking his love for this town or his aspirations for the lodge.

She wanted to see those aspirations come to fruition. She wanted him to achieve his dreams. And the best way to do that was to close the deal on the manuscript so he had the necessary working capital. But closing the deal would also mean it was time for her to go back to LA, and strangely enough, she wasn't ready to leave.

When had that changed?

Karen Sullivan stood, pulling Maddie from her private thoughts.

"It's time I put this little one and myself down for a nap," Karen said. "What about you, Grandpa? Care to join us?"

"Can't," her husband answered. "I've challenged Cookie to a game of chess."

From the kitchen, Cookie called, "He'll wish he'd chosen that nap after I've whupped him."

Everyone laughed.

With the meal at an end, Audrey bid everyone a pleasant day before leaving to visit a friend for the afternoon. Tony rose from his chair and began clearing dishes from the table. Karen disappeared up the stairs with Iris in her arms while Sam headed for the reading room to set up the chessboard. Within minutes, everyone but Maddie was gone from the dining room.

She felt at loose ends. She could go to her room and take a nap like Karen and Iris or she could get her book to read or she could open her laptop and go over some business items. Only she didn't want to. She wanted to stay with Tony.

She grabbed her crutches and made her way to the kitchen. Pushing the swinging door open before her, she asked, "Would you like some help with the dishes? I could dry."

Tony glanced over his shoulder, then turned off the running water. "I'm sorry. What did you say?"

"I offered to help, if you'd like."

"No thanks. Guests of the lodge aren't required to wash their dishes." He grinned. "We're laid back, but not that laid back. Unless, of course, you can't pay your bill. Then we might have to put you to work."

"I'm not a paying guest." She entered the kitchen, and the door swung closed behind her. "My room is complimentary. Remember?"

"True." His eyes narrowed as he looked at her. "But I bet you should rest and keep that foot up."

"I'm fine. It's not hurting at all." Okay, that was a slight fib. There was some discomfort, but nothing to make a fuss over.

Tony held up a dishtowel. "All right. If you're sure."

"I'm sure." She maneuvered her way around the center island to the right side of the sink. "I wanted to thank you for inviting me to church. I loved the service, and your pastor is wonderful."

"Yeah, we're blessed to have a man like Luke leading our congregation. I think his teaching is anointed. Dozens of churches would want to hire him in a second if he decided to leave Cloud Mountain."

"There were times this morning when I felt as if he was speaking just to me."

Tony smiled. "It's great when the Holy Spirit does that, isn't it?"

"Yes."

But I haven't felt that way in a long time. Have I been keeping God at arm's length? Have I closed my ears to His Spirit?

Maddie wasn't ready to explore those questions, so she asked another of Tony. "Where's Cookie?"

"He went to change his clothes before the big chess match. He doesn't find a willing victim very often."

"He's good?"

Tony nodded. "He's *good*."

Maddie set the crutches aside and leaned her hip against the counter, dishtowel ready. "You three are like family, aren't you? You and Audrey and Cookie."

"Yeah, we are. I might own the place, but they want it to succeed as much as I do."

"I know Cookie lives here in the lodge, but what about Audrey?"

"She has her own house about a quarter mile down the road."

As he talked, Tony filled the sink with hot water, the dish soap piling high above the surface. "She stays overnight here when she needs to, but that doesn't happen often. Eventually, we'll hire more full-time help. God willing, the day we need more help will come soon."

Selling the manuscript will help you make it happen. David wants it and is willing to pay. We could close the deal this afternoon.

Tony placed some dirty dishes in the sink, and soap bubbles flew into the air in small clusters. One bunch landed on Maddie's nose. Before she could brush at it with her hand, Tony leaned toward her and blew the bubbles away.

Her breathing slowed. Her heartbeat doubled. She felt a little lightheaded.

Tony took the dishtowel from her, dried his hands, and then clasped her shoulders, as if afraid she might crumple to the floor. Only that wasn't why his hands gripped her arms.

He held her as a prelude to a kiss.

His lips were warm, the pressure light and tender. He smelled of a musky cologne and wood smoke. The two combined made for a heady, masculine scent. She breathed it in, savoring the smell of him, the taste of him.

All too soon, Tony drew back, ending the kiss. She looked at him and saw questions in his eyes, questions for which she had no answers. She only knew she wanted him to kiss her again, to go on kissing her and never stop.

Don't stop. Don't stop.

Tony cleared his throat and drew back a little further. "Maybe we'd better get these dishes washed."

It felt like a rejection. Perhaps it shouldn't, but it did.

"Yes," she whispered. "I guess we should."

"Maddie ..."

She looked down at the dishtowel in her hand. "Let's not talk about it, Tony. It's better we stick to business. Don't you think?"

He didn't reply.

That was answer enough for Maddie.

CHAPTER 11

*H*e shouldn't have kissed her. It was too soon. He'd moved too fast.

Okay, so he'd had a crush on her a decade ago. A crush so strong he even remembered she liked hot tea with milk instead of lemon. But it wasn't as if they'd dated. She hadn't known him from Adam. Not really. Not until a few days ago.

And even if she *did* know him from Adam, what future was there for the two of them? She lived in LA. He lived in Cloud Mountain. If two more different places existed in America, he didn't know what they were. La-la-land and the backwoods. Why would he think she'd want to live here? And there was no way he wanted to return to a big city.

But if he made the improvements in the lodge, if their ski resort could begin competing with some of the others in Idaho, if ...

If ... if ... if ...

Maddie finished drying the dishes, but Tony could tell she no longer wanted to be there. As soon as the last pot was done, she excused herself and beat a hasty retreat.

Why was I so stupid? Why didn't I keep my head?

Because he loved her.

There. It was that simple. He loved her. Maybe it didn't make sense. Maybe it happened too fast. But that's how he felt. He loved her.

With his palms pressed against the counter, he bowed his head. *Lord, help me out here. I'm feeling confused, and I don't know what to do next.*

He waited. Waited for God's voice to speak to his heart. Waited for a flash of inspiration. Waited to be overwhelmed by the knowledge of what he should say or do. He waited, but none of those things happened.

He wished life as a Christian were easier sometimes. There were many things spelled out in the Bible, but who to love, who to marry, wasn't one of them. There was no verse that said, "Tony Anderson, Maddie Scott is the girl for you." Be nice if there was.

He opened his eyes and looked out the window. It was snowing. The forecast had said they could get from six to ten inches before tomorrow morning. It looked like the weatherman had it right this time.

After a quick glance around the kitchen to make sure all was as it should be—lest he get on Cookie's bad side—he headed for the reading room to see how the chess match was going. If Cookie didn't win, they'd *all* be on his bad side for the next couple of days.

He stopped at the entrance to the room, unnoticed by either of the older men. Both Sam and Cookie stared at the chessboard, frowns of concentration furrowing their brows.

Better not disturb them, Tony decided. He turned on his heel and walked to his office where he awakened his computer from sleep mode. A short while later, he scanned the messages in his email program's inbox, including a number of queries about the lodge and the surrounding area. Couldn't have too many of those. There was also an email from a cousin and some general business correspondence that needed attention. He might as well tackle them all.

An hour later, Tony hit *send* on his final reply and leaned back in his desk chair, stretching his arms over his head to work out the kinks. He supposed now would be a good time to have his meeting with Maddie. Only he wasn't sure—

The phone rang and he reached for it. "Cloud Mountain Lodge."

"Tony. It's Frank Martin."

"Hey, Doc. Calling to check on your patient?" He had his finger poised to send the call through to Maddie's room.

"No. We've got some missing skiers."

Tony straightened. "Who?" The faces of his guests flashed before his eyes. Had something happened to one of the Sullivans?

"Gary Patterson and his girlfriend, Nancy Barrett. They went cross-country skiing with some other young folk this morning. Those two fell behind and never made it to the rendezvous point."

Gary hadn't lived in Cloud Mountain much longer than Tony, but he was a good skier. Nancy had lived here most of her life and knew her way around these mountains. Both were smart enough to take shelter from the storm if they had to.

"We're organizing a search," Frank added.

He stood. "What do you need from me?"

"There's a couple different ways they might have gone. I'm going with Chuck Barrett to Snake Flats. Can you take your snowcat up the logging road to Frazier Ridge?"

"Of course."

"Meet us at the Dry Creek parking lot. We'll coordinate from there."

"I'm on my way." Tony dropped the handset into its cradle and turned as Audrey appeared in the doorway.

"Did you hear about Nancy and Gary?" she asked.

"Yes. I'm headed up to Frazier Ridge in the snowcat."

"I'll put together some blankets and a couple of thermos bottles of hot coffee." Audrey looked at her wristwatch. "You have about three hours of daylight left."

"Is it still snowing?"

"Yes. It's bad out there. I had a dickens of a time getting back to the lodge. Couldn't see much past the hood of the car."

In other words, no time to waste. While Audrey went to the kitchen to prepare the thermoses, Tony headed for his private quarters to change into attire more suitable to blizzard conditions. By the time he returned, Cookie, Sam, and Maddie had joined Audrey in the lobby. Karen was there, too, sitting on a wooden chair, holding Iris on her lap.

"Audrey told us what happened," Maddie said. "What can we do to help?"

"Pray. Pray hard."

"Shouldn't someone go with you?" Her eyes were filled with worry.

He shook his head. "No, I'll be okay. I've got a radio in the cat. I can call for help if I need it." He felt the urge to hug Maddie. He'd love to fold her in his arms and kiss her once before he left.

"I put the thermoses and blankets by the back door," Audrey said. "Don't forget to grab some extra flashlights. Cookie and I will whip up some grub in case any search teams bring the skiers here."

"Thanks, Audrey. Hopefully we'll all be back before nightfall."

God, guide us to Nancy and Gary. Protect them until help arrives.

TONY HADN'T BEEN GONE MORE than ten minutes when footsteps on the front porch drew all eyes toward the door. Moments later, the rest of the Sullivans tromped into the lobby.

"Oh, thank heaven!" Karen dashed into the lobby and began hugging her children and grandchildren, one after another. "I was getting worried. Why didn't you get off that mountain when the storm began?"

Her oldest son, Mike, gave her a puzzled look. "It wasn't all that bad until thirty minutes ago."

Audrey said, "We've got some cross-country skiers lost in the storm. It's made everyone anxious."

"We hadn't heard. Sorry, Mom." Mike put his arm around Karen's shoulders and gave her a squeeze. "We're all okay. Sorry we worried you."

Maddie went into the reading room, but she was too restless to sit down. Instead she leaned against her crutches while staring out the window. Not that she could see anything but a flurry of white.

Please, God. Protect everyone who is out there searching. Protect those who are lost. Guide their way. Make the pathways clear.

She drew a shuddery breath.

Please protect Tony. Bring him back to the lodge, safe and sound. Bring him back to ...

Tears welled in her eyes.

... to me.

She closed her eyes, recalling the kiss they'd shared. Only in her imagination he didn't pull away so soon. This time his lips lingered on hers.

He remembered I preferred tea to coffee. After all these years ...

She looked out at the storm again, the snow whirling and spinning past the window, resembling how she felt on the inside—confused, tossed about by a strong wind, saddened over what might have been. Tony's life was here. Hers was in California.

"Don't worry about him, Maddie."

She looked to her right where Audrey now stood.

"Tony knows this country from his boyhood, and he's trekked all over it since he moved here last spring. He's no flatlander. He'll keep his wits about him."

Pride wanted Maddie to deny she was worried about Tony. Honesty wouldn't allow it. She turned her gaze out the window again. "I haven't seen snow like this in a long, long time." She shook her head. "I suppose you'd call me a flatlander."

"Mmm. Maybe. Maybe not. I've got a feeling you'd fit in around here rather nicely." She patted Maddie on the shoulder. "I'd best get back to the kitchen and give Cookie a hand."

What if Audrey was right? What if Maddie *would* fit in around there rather nicely? Was it crazy to want to?

Was it crazy to want Tony?

Tony had almost reached the top end of the logging road on Frazier Ridge when word came over the radio that the two missing skiers had been found and were okay. They were cold and hungry but uninjured. Tony said a quick prayer of thanksgiving as he turned the snowcat around and headed for home.

Alone in the cab, staring at the snowy white world beyond the headlights and listening to the steady rumbling of the engine, Tony allowed his thoughts to return to Maddie. This emergency had postponed their second meeting about the manuscript, but Tony couldn't count on anything else happening to give him more time to win her affections. Oh, he might delay a little if he pretended to consider other offers, but that would be a lie. He already knew he wanted David to have it.

"Father, I can't think of anything else to do. I want her to come to know me better, to learn to care for me the way I care for her. She could be gone in a few days, and then I might never see her again. So if she's the woman You have in store for me, You're going to have to do something."

He glanced out at the storm.

Maybe Your plan is to snow her in.

He smiled at the thought. It wasn't a farfetched idea. After all, God had been known to stop the sun in its tracks, to dry up the rains, and to part the sea. Why not send a blizzard to throw two people together if that's what He wanted?

But the real question remained—was this what God wanted? Had He brought Maddie here for this purpose?

"Make it clear to both of us, Father."

Tony thought of himself as a levelheaded sort. He wasn't one to give into sudden whims. He was more methodical in his approach to both life and business. Buying this lodge had been something he'd done with careful planning and forethought. He'd saved and researched and never rushed a decision.

But there was nothing levelheaded or methodical about his feelings for Maddie. The moment he first saw her standing in the lobby of the lodge, he'd felt his life was about to change.

As he drew closer to town, lights from the lodge shown through the curtain of snow like a golden beacon, welcoming him back. It made him feel good, seeing those lights and knowing everything they represented. The lodge was home to him, but it was also hope for the community. As the lodge prospered, so would other businesses in town. More skiers in the winter, more vacationers in the summer, meant more dollars flowing into Cloud Mountain, dollars that would find their way into the schools and the fire department and the police department.

With everything in him, he wanted the lodge to succeed. He was willing to work hard to make it happen. And he'd been willing to do it alone. He'd been on his own all his adult life. He was used to the single life, and while he'd hoped he would one day meet the woman who was meant to be his wife, he hadn't been impatient or unhappy. He'd believed love would happen in God's good and perfect time.

Was this His good and perfect time? Was Maddie the woman he'd waited for?

He hoped so … because this sure felt like love.

CHAPTER 12

*M*addie didn't sleep well. Her dreams were troubled, and when she awakened from them, she felt as if she'd run a marathon during the night. Her muscles ached. Her ankle throbbed.

She rolled onto her side and looked at the digital clock on the nightstand. It wasn't yet six o'clock. She rolled to her other side and closed her eyes, willing herself to go back to sleep. Instead, Tony's image drifted into her mind.

After his return last night, while everyone in the lodge rejoiced over the safe return of the lost skiers, Maddie had caught him watching her, a frown pinching his forehead. Had she done something to displease him? If so, she couldn't think what.

With a sigh of exasperation, she flopped onto her back and stared upward. "Close the deal and go home. If you leave now, you'll be all right. You don't need a man in your life. You don't need to fall in love again. You just need to pay off your debts so you can stop worrying about them."

But if that's true, why does my heart hurt when I think of not seeing him again?

In the darkness of her room, she pictured Tony. She remembered him on the first day she arrived, recalled that vague sense that she should know him. She remembered how he'd carefully coached her on the bunny hill, his words of encouragement as they rode the ski lift, his concern for her when she fell. She envisioned him chopping wood and that fluttery feeling watching him had stirred in her heart. She remembered the sound of his voice lifted in worship. She recalled his infectious laughter.

Maddie grabbed a pillow and pressed it over her face as the memory of Tony's lips upon hers invaded her senses. Oh, that kiss. That wonderfully torturous sweet kiss. If only it could have gone on longer. If only he'd kissed her again and again and again.

She released a pent-up groan and tossed aside the pillow, then sat up in bed. After switching on the lamp, she reached for her robe. A few minutes later, she made her way out of her room, down the hall, and through the dining room. Hopefully a cup of tea would soothe her thoughts. Of course, first she had to find where Cookie kept things in the kitchen.

The teakettle was easy. It was on the stove. She managed to take it to the sink and fill it with water while still supporting herself with her crutches. As she turned, kettle in hand, the kitchen door swung open.

Tony—clad in Levi's and blue plaid shirt—stood in the doorway, his hair mussed from sleep, surprise widening his eyes. "Maddie?"

"I'm sorry. Did I wake you?"

"No. I'm usually the first one up. Starting the coffee brewing is my job."

She raised the kettle in her hand. "I wanted some tea."

"Here." He strode toward her. "Let me help you with that." He took the teakettle, set it on a burner, and turned the knob on the stove. Looking back at her, he motioned with his head toward a stool. "Sit down and relax. It won't take long for the water to heat."

Maddie was glad to oblige. It allowed her the pleasure of watching him as he moved about the kitchen.

"Mind a little music?" he asked as he reached for a boom box and pressed the play button without waiting for an answer.

"It's beginning to look a lot like Christmas," a male voice sang through the speakers.

Tony joined in on the next line, tossing a grin in Maddie's direction, a silent invitation to sing along.

Her heart stuttered in response. She couldn't have sung a note to save her soul.

"Where will you spend Christmas, Maddie? Will you join your mom and sister in Florida?"

"Not this year."

She hadn't spent Christmas with her family in ages. When she was married, it was because Craig always had somewhere else he wanted to be. After the divorce, it was too painful to be with her sister and brother-in-law. The two were blissfully happy, as much in love today as when they'd wed fifteen years ago, and seeing them made her feel a bit sorry for herself.

She pointed at her ankle. "Good thing I didn't plan to go. I'd hate to be flying across the country with this."

Tony leaned a hip against the counter and crossed his arms over his chest. "I'm sorry about that. I shouldn't have encouraged you to go on the ski lift. We could have kept using the rope tow and stayed to the smaller hill."

"It isn't your fault."

"It feels like it." He was silent for a short while before saying, "Why don't you stay here at the lodge for Christmas?"

"Here?" Her heart skipped again.

"Why not? Doc says you shouldn't drive for a while. I'll bet David would agree with me that you should stay put."

Now her heart was racing. "I didn't bring enough clothes."

"That wouldn't be too hard to fix. Nobody should spend Christmas alone. Besides, you shouldn't miss the feast Cookie will prepare."

Did he ask because he wanted her to stay? Or did he feel sorry for her because she was far from family at Christmas?

The teakettle began to whistle, and Tony pushed off the counter and walked to the stove. "Think about it, Maddie," he said as he poured water into a cup.

She was quite certain she would think of little else.

~

"YOU'VE HAD a silly grin on your face ever since I got here this morning." Audrey set a stack of mail on Tony's desk. "What are you so happy about?"

"Nothing in particular." His smile widened. He couldn't help it. He'd been a grinning fool ever since he talked to Maddie that morning. The idea of her staying at the lodge over the holidays had popped into his head suddenly, and before he knew it, he'd said it aloud. He figured that had to be a good thing. Maybe even a God thing.

"I know you better than that, Tony. Fess up."

"I asked Maddie to stay here for Christmas. At the lodge with all of us."

Audrey cocked an eyebrow. "And she's going to?"

"She didn't say yes yet, but she didn't say no either."

"I had a feeling about you and that young woman."

"Me, too."

Audrey turned toward the office door. "While you're in such a good mood, you might want to think about ordering wallpaper for some of the rooms in the east wing. We got another reservation today, and I'd hate to have to turn anybody down because enough rooms aren't ready."

Tony leaned back in his chair. *Thanks, Lord.* Too many reservations was a problem he looked forward to.

He swiveled around and pulled a binder off the bookshelf. Inside the hard blue covers were his plans and projections for the lodge, figures and ideas that went back several years. He opened it on his desk and flipped through the pages.

Two hundred thousand dollars.

New roof. Remodeled kitchen. Update the heating and air conditioning system. What else could he do with that amount of money? And how much higher might Fairchild be willing to go?

Tony turned another page in the binder.

Even with all the remodeling and restoring, could the lodge provide the sort of life Maddie wanted? She was a city girl. Cloud Mountain, even with a nice lodge, would still be Cloud Mountain. Would she be happy here?

His smile was replaced with a frown.

God, have I gotten ahead of You?

He rose from the chair and walked out of his office. The lodge was quiet again. Most of the Sullivan clan were skiing or snow-boarding, eager to test the fresh powder from the previous night's storm. Those who weren't on the mountain had gone into town to browse in the different tourist shops that lined Main Street.

Where was Maddie? Had she gone to town as well?

As if in answer, he heard laughter—Maddie's laughter—coming from the kitchen. He followed the irresistible sound, and what he found was equally irresistible. Maddie, a smudge of flour on one cheek and another on the tip of her nose, rolling out cookie dough, her right knee resting on the seat of a chair. Cookie stood nearby, stirring something bright green in a mixing bowl.

"Ah, Tony," the chef said. "Have you come to help us?"

"Depends. What are you making?"

"Christmas cookies, of course." He held up the bowl. "Here's the frosting for the trees."

Tony crossed the kitchen and stopped on the other side of the table where Maddie was now pressing various shaped cutters into the dough. "You look like you're having a good time."

"I am." She plucked up a piece of dough and popped it into her mouth, then closed her eyes. "Mmmm. I haven't eaten cookie dough in years."

When she looked at him again, the sparkle of joy in her brown eyes nearly took his breath away. He remembered all too well the sadness that had filled them on the day she arrived.

"Here," she said, holding a spoonful of cookie dough toward him. "Indulge."

Nothing on earth could have stopped him from doing her bidding, and he didn't even *like* cookie dough.

"Good, huh?"

He swallowed the sugary gob of flour, eggs, and vanilla. "Mmm. Good." Hopefully, lightning wouldn't strike him dead for telling a lie. *But please don't offer me another bite.*

"When I was a little girl, my mom and sister and I would spend one Saturday in December baking and frosting sugar cookies. My hands would be stained red and blue and green from the food coloring. Oh, and the little candies we sprinkled on top. I loved eating those, too. When I got older, I looked forward to the day I could revive the tradition with my own children."

And just like that, her smile was gone.

Why didn't you and Craig have kids?

Tears welled in her eyes as she answered the question he hadn't asked aloud. "Craig always said he wasn't ready to be a dad." She shrugged. "But I guess that's changed now."

He reached out and touched her cheek with his fingertips. "You deserve better, Maddie." *I'd give you better.*

The hint of a smile returned to her lips as she blinked away the tears. "Thanks. I didn't mean to go all weepy on you." She waved the spoon in the air. "Must be too much sugar."

"Yeah. Must be."

She watched him in silence, and Tony found himself wishing he could read her thoughts. He didn't want to frighten her off. He wanted her to feel safe with him. How could he prove that he wouldn't hurt her the way Craig had?

"Tony," Cookie said, "if you aren't going to help, leave. You're interfering with my workforce."

Maddie laughed as she handed Tony the rolling pin. "Best do as he says. You roll. I'll cut."

If it meant he could spend more time with her, he was happy to oblige.

CHAPTER 13

On Tuesday, Tony and Maddie finished their negotiations for the manuscript, agreeing to a slightly higher amount than the original offer. Everyone involved was pleased. Tony because he could speed up renovations to the lodge. Maddie because she would soon be debt-free. David because he was adding something he prized to his collection.

"The contract of sale will arrive at the lodge by Friday," David told Maddie when they talked later that day.

"Good. I'll tell Tony to expect it. I know he'll be glad when everything is signed, sealed, and delivered."

"So when are you flying back to LA?"

She worried her lower lip.

"Maddie? Did I lose you?"

"No, I'm here. I ... well, I'm not sure when I'm flying back. Tony invited me to stay at the lodge through Christmas."

"That's a great idea."

"I haven't decided yet."

"I think you should."

She stared at the red boot on her ankle, braced on the foot-stool in her guest room. "You do?"

"Yes, I do. Remember the advice I gave you when you first arrived?"

"Uh-huh. Have fun, you said. It's thanks to your advice that I'm on crutches."

"But you want to stay, don't you?"

She thought of Tony's sweet kiss two days ago. Why hadn't he tried to kiss her again? She'd wanted him to. And yesterday when she'd fed him the cookie dough, she'd thought—

"Maddie, you do want to stay, don't you?"

"Yes."

"Then stay."

"My mail must be a mile high by now."

"Nothing that can't wait a couple of weeks."

"You make me feel expendable."

"You're not expendable, Maddie, but I would like to see you happy. Really happy. I don't think you're going to find happiness through your work."

To be honest, neither did she.

"Sorry, Maddie. I've got a call on the other line I need to take. Let me know when the contracts get there."

"I will."

"Goodbye."

"Bye."

She closed her cell phone, breaking the connection.

"I think you should stay."

Maddie *could* use a real holiday, and it would be fun to spend Christmas with everyone at the lodge. She may not have known Tony, Audrey or Cookie for long, but she was fond of them, all the same.

Perhaps more than fond of Tony.

∾

STANDING in the center of the Uriah Small guest room, Tony

imagined different possibilities for it. This room needed to be more than a place for guests to sleep. After all, by leaving behind that manuscript, Mr. Small was responsible for Tony's dreams for the lodge coming to fruition all the sooner.

Maybe he should turn it into a library, although he supposed that wasn't a good idea. It was too far from the center of activity.

Maybe he should make this room part of a suite. This could be the sitting room, and the guest room next door could be the bedroom. It would be easy enough to put a door in the connecting wall. He could buy some used editions of Uriah Small's works to fill the bookcase, and once David Fairchild had the manuscript published, they could give the new work a place of honor.

"Knock, knock."

Maddie's voice drew him around to face the door.

"Audrey told me you were up here." She swung herself into the room.

"I was going over some possibilities in my head."

"Is this the room where you found the manuscript?"

"Yeah." He pointed toward the wall. "Right over there. Sometimes I can't believe how the Lord blessed me with that find. Others could have found it long before I got here."

"What if you hadn't found it?"

He considered the question a moment before answering, "It wouldn't have changed all that much. Except how long it would take before I finish the remodeling." He smiled. "Oh, and Cookie will be happier with that new kitchen he's about to get."

She laughed softly. "He was telling me about that yesterday. He'll be in seventh heaven."

Should he ask her if she'd decided to stay for Christmas? Or should he be patient and let her tell him in her own good time? How could he know which was the right way? He wasn't afraid of risks in his business life. If he were, he wouldn't be the owner of this lodge. But he didn't want to risk losing Maddie.

"I talked to David a short while ago. He said he'll have the contracts delivered to you by Friday."

"Great." *Unless that means you'll be leaving.*

"Are you planning to do something special with this room?" She used her crutches to draw closer to Tony.

"That's what I was thinking. Something special. But I'm not sure what."

"This would make a lovely living room for a suite." She moved to one of the windows. "You can see the town from here and the mountain from over there."

He wanted to hold her and kiss her, if for no other reason than she'd matched his own idea for the room. Except there were other reasons. Lots of them. He was hungry to take her in his arms, to tell her he loved her, to ask her to stay so that they could talk about every change made to the lodge, so he could hear her ideas, so they could plan things together.

She looked at him again.

A man could drown in her eyes.

"Tony, I'd like to accept your invitation to stay at the lodge through Christmas."

He stepped toward her. *Say something. Tell her you're glad she's going to stay.*

"It will be a nice change from LA. I haven't seen a white Christmas in ten years at least."

"I guarantee it'll be white." He reached out and cupped the side of her face with his hand.

She leaned into his touch, a movement so slight he wasn't sure it happened.

He spoke her name on a breath.

She smiled.

Ker-thump went his heart. He was growing used to it by now.

From the end of the hall, Audrey's voice intruded on the moment. "Tony, you're needed on the telephone."

"Can you take a message?" he called back, not wanting to move, not wanting to think, not wanting to breathe.

"He says it's important."

Maddie drew back. "You'd better take it."

"Wait here. I won't be long. We can talk over a few more ideas for this room."

She nodded, her smile tenuous.

Tony turned on his heel and strode from the room. Whoever was on the phone would be sorry if what they had to say wasn't important.

He took the stairs two at a time, entered his office, and yanked the phone from its cradle. "Tony Anderson speaking."

"Mr. Anderson," the voice on the other end of the line said, "my name is Phillip Endicott. I represent Mariah Kent. Ms. Kent is the great-niece of Uriah Small and the legal heir to his estate."

With those last few words, Tony felt the bottom drop out of his world.

"Ms. Kent recently learned that you've discovered some of her uncle's last remaining work."

"Yes."

"I'm sure you'll understand that she is eager to have the property returned to her."

Returned to her.

No contract to sign with David Fairchild.

No discussions about how to turn the room upstairs into the Uriah Small suite.

No money to speed things along.

No new roof.

No new kitchen.

Just like that, back to square one.

Tony said something about having his attorney contact Mr. Endicott, asked for a little more information, and hung up the phone.

God, what are You doing?

He sank onto his desk chair. Five years. His original plan had called for it to take at least five years to finish the work on the lodge and begin to turn a profit. And there might not ever be a large profit. Enough but not a lot. Enough for him but maybe not enough for a wife and family. Maybe not for Maddie.

She deserves better than I have to offer.

With a heavy heart, he picked up the telephone and dialed the number for his attorney.

CHAPTER 14

*T*he mood around the lodge was subdued in the days following that fateful phone call. Even the Sullivans were affected by the news.

"Maybe you can fight this," Sam Sullivan told Tony. "If there's anything I can do, I'd be glad to help. It seems wrong that this woman can take the manuscript after you found it."

"If she's the rightful heir, she should have it." It pained Tony to say those words, but he knew they were true. "All I can do now is wait and see what my attorney advises. But thanks for the offer. I appreciate it."

Sam wasn't the only person offering help, advice, and sympathy—or all three. As word spread, the citizens of Cloud Mountain showed up at the lodge. Pastor Luke came to pray with Tony. Evie Barrett brought sweets from the candy store. Gary Patterson and his sister, Betina, offered to lend a hand with wallpaper hanging or painting or whatever else he might need. And there were others who came, many others, all of them asking what they could do.

Tony appreciated the expressions of kindness more than he

could say, but while the loss of the manuscript—and what that could have meant for the lodge—was a great disappointment, it was knowing he had nothing much to offer Maddie that broke his heart. For a brief while, he'd harbored hope that she might choose Cloud Mountain over LA, choose managing a lodge over closing deals for David Fairchild, choose a small country church for one with thousands of members.

That she might choose me.

Now his hopes seemed as fleeting as a dream.

MADDIE OBSERVED the show of concern from Tony's friends and wished she could be one of them. But something happened on the day he took that phone call. He'd erected an invisible wall between them, and Maddie didn't know how to tear it down.

"I don't know, David." Lying on her back on the bed, she stared at the ceiling of her guest room. "Maybe I should come home for Christmas after all. I could hire someone to drive me to Boise so I could turn in the rental car and catch a flight to LA. There doesn't seem to be much reason to stay here now."

"What do you mean, Maddie?"

"Well, with the rightful ownership of the manuscript up in the air, we can't close the deal and—"

"Wait. You weren't going to stay because of business. You were going to stay because Tony asked you to. You were going to make a holiday of it."

Her chest felt as if it were being squeezed by an iron band.

David's voice hardened. "He didn't take back the invitation, did he?"

"No, but—"

"Then why leave?"

Tears slipped from her eyes, leaving damp tracks along her

temples and into her hair. "Because I don't think Tony wants me here. I'm a reminder of what he almost had but lost, of all the things he won't be able to do with the lodge for now."

"If that's true, he isn't the man I thought he was. But I'm betting it isn't true. Don't run away, Maddie."

How could she tell David that she was afraid to stay? She knew too well what it was like to love someone who didn't love her in return. She never wanted to experience that pain again.

Only, deep down, she knew it was too late to escape the pain. She'd already fallen in love with Tony Anderson. With Tony and this lodge and Audrey and Cookie. With the quaint little town and the people who lived in it. With Redeemer Community Church and the Candy Corner and the medical clinic. Even with that miserable spot on the mountain where she'd broken her ankle.

"Think about it, Maddie, and call me again tomorrow."

"Okay," she whispered, her throat too tight for much sound.

As soon as she closed the phone, she rolled onto her side and curled into a ball, praying the ache in her heart would stop soon.

TONY DROVE the snowcat along the same road he and his guests had taken in Nick Robertson's sleigh the previous week. Only now the sun shone in a clear sky overhead, and the light reflected off the snow as if from a million diamonds. At the lookout point at the top of the hill, he pulled into the parking lot and cut the engine. Silence enveloped the cab.

He stared down at the picture-postcard view of Cloud Mountain, remembering how long he'd planned for the day that he could move here to live. He'd wanted it. He'd worked for it.

Now there was something—some*one*—he wanted even more. What was he going to do about Maddie?

In the stillness of the snowy hilltop, he thought of Jacob and Rebekah from the Bible. Jacob had loved Rebekah so much he worked for seven years to gain her hand in marriage, and after being tricked by her father, he worked another seven.

What are you ready to do to win Maddie's love?

Would he work for seven years?

Yes.

Would he give up the lodge and Cloud Mountain?

He held his breath, unsure what his heart would answer.

Yes, I would.

It surprised him, the certainty he felt, but it was true. If he had to, he would follow Maddie to California. He would return to the corporate treadmill. If that's what it took, he was willing.

He loved her that much.

He started the snowcat's engine and turned the vehicle toward town.

AUDREY STEPPED from behind the desk in the lobby. "I'm not sure where Tony went, but he took the snowcat. He may be out for a while. Is there something I can do for you?"

"No." Maddie took a deep breath and released it. "I've been thinking I'd ask one of the Sullivans to drive me to Boise in my rental car on Sunday since they'll be going that way themselves."

"But Tony said you were staying for Christmas."

"I was, but ..." She shrugged. "I'm not certain I should now."

"Well, *I'm* certain," the woman replied, emphasizing her words with an abrupt nod of her head.

Maddie gave her a tremulous smile. "Thanks, Audrey."

Then she turned away, not wanting to risk the return of her tears. It already felt as if she were saying goodbye to too much. She decided to go to her room to begin packing. Even though she would be here a couple more days, it didn't hurt to get an early start.

She had almost arrived at her room when the back door

opened and Tony stepped into view. Maddie's heart tripped at the sight of him.

If only …

"Maddie, would you take a ride with me in the snowcat?"

She should say no. Being near him was too hard. What she said was, "Okay."

"Great." He smiled, and her heart tripped again. "Where's your coat?"

"In here." She slid the key card into the reader and opened the door to her room. "I'll get it."

"I'll wait."

She didn't know what this was about. She didn't care, not if it was responsible for making him smile again.

A short while later, Tony carried her out to the snowcat and deposited her on the passenger seat of the cab before running around to the driver side and hopping in.

"Where are we going?"

He started the engine. "Just up the hill a ways. It won't take us long to get there."

More questions swirled in her mind, but she didn't ask them. She decided to enjoy the interlude. It would be over all too soon. Reality would come crashing in, and by Sunday, she would say goodbye to Tony.

But not yet. It wasn't here yet.

She patted the side panel of the door. "This is really something. I've never been in a snowcat before."

"Not much use for them in LA."

"No." She looked out the window. Here was one more thing she would miss. "I suppose not."

"I got a good deal on this one. It's come in handy more than once this winter."

I don't want to talk about the snowcat. I want to tell you how much I care about you. I want to tell you I've lost my heart to you. I want to ask you to kiss me again and to hold me close and never let me go.

"Look." Tony pointed toward the edge of the forest. "A fox." Maddie followed the direction of his hand but all she saw was a flash of reddish brown as it disappeared into the trees.

"In the summer, we get lots of deer and elk in these parts. When I was a kid, my aunt and uncle had trouble with a bear that thought their garbage can was his personal smorgasbord. Man, my aunt would get so angry when she had to clean up the mess that bear left behind."

"Where was their cabin?"

"Back the other side of town about two and a half miles."

The snowcat climbed a hillside, rumbling and grumbling along. Maddie thought this must be a lot like riding in a tank, except without suffering from claustrophobia. The cat had plenty of windows. At the top of the hill, Tony turned the vehicle into a parking area and came to a halt a few feet before reaching the guardrail. Then he turned off the engine.

The silence was so complete it startled Maddie. She held her breath, not wanting to disturb it.

"I came up here to think awhile ago," Tony said. "I was thinking about all the stuff I couldn't do without that manuscript to sell."

"I'm so sorry."

"No. Listen, Maddie. I have something I need to say to you." He pointed again. "Look down there. See the town? That's the kind of place I want to live. The people who have been coming by the lodge all week? They're the kind of people I want for my friends and neighbors."

She nodded, understanding why he felt that way. She felt it too, and she'd been here only a short while.

"But Maddie?"

Something about his tone—soft, gentle, almost like a caress— caused her to turn her head to look at him.

"There's something I want far more than the lodge or this town or my friends and neighbors."

Blood began to pound in her ears. "There is?"

"You, Maddie. I want you." He cupped her chin with his hand. "I love you. Some might think it happened too fast. Maybe you think it's too fast. But my feelings are real."

Tears caused his image to swim before her eyes.

"I know you've got debts to pay, and I know the lodge won't make us lots of money. It'll take time before it's able to turn much of a profit. I think we could manage, but success won't happen overnight. So if you need to go back to California, then I'm willing to come there. I'm willing to do whatever it takes for us to be together. Just let me know if I've got a ghost of a chance to win your love."

Something happened in that moment. It was as if fear had been cut from her heart, leaving room for trust to move in. Maybe God had been working that miracle from the start of her trip to Idaho, but it was completed in the cab of this snowcat on a hillside overlooking Cloud Mountain.

Awed by the wonder of it all, she shook her head from side to side as the tears fell from her eyes, streaking her cheeks.

"Not even a chance, Maddie?"

She blinked back more tears. "No, that isn't what I meant. Tony, I couldn't ask you to leave Cloud Mountain." She drew a quick breath. "I don't want to leave either. Not ever. And I … I don't want to leave you."

Tony's hands cradled her face as they drew closer to each other. Their lips met, and she tasted the salt of her tears. The kiss ended, but they didn't draw back. They remained close, their foreheads almost touching.

"Maddie, I pledge to you my faithfulness. As God is my witness, I'll never be untrue to you."

She believed him. With nothing held back, she believed in his love and his faithfulness and his steadfastness. She didn't need him or anyone to tell her that he spoke the truth. She believed him at the very center of her heart, a place once abandoned but now filled to overflowing with joy.

December was once again her favorite month.

EPILOGUE

Christmas Morning, one year later

addie glanced at the clock on the nightstand. It was only 4:30, but she was wide awake. Upstairs in the east wing, her mom slept in one of the guest rooms, while a few doors down the hall from her, in the Uriah Small suite, David and Lois did the same. Before breakfast, they would all gather in the reading room to open Christmas gifts, but that was still a few hours away.

And it wasn't the anticipation of opening presents that made her sleepless. It was something far better.

"Merry Christmas," Tony whispered, his voice low and gravely. "Can't sleep?"

She couldn't see her husband in the darkness of the bedroom, but she didn't need to see him to know that he slept on his back, one arm flung over his head. Not after six months as his wife.

She turned onto her side and laid her head on his shoulder. "No, I can't sleep."

"Were you like this as a kid? Can I expect this every Christmas morning?"

"Yes. I'm always the first one awake on Christmas morning."

"Hmm. I've always been the one who slept in."

"That'll never do." She laughed softly. "Besides, I'm surprised you could sleep at all after David's big news. Can you believe he's put together that group to invest in the resort in such a short amount of time? Another lift. A snowmaking machine. Some condos. I knew he liked it here in Cloud Mountain, but I didn't know how much."

"Yeah." There was a smile in his voice now. "I'll bet the news has already traveled from one end of town to the other. This is going to mean lots of new jobs."

"You know ..." She lifted her head to kiss him on the cheek. "Maybe we'll have so many guests staying at the lodge that we'll have to think about moving out and into a house of our own."

"That would be great. Maybe next year or the one after. Things won't change overnight."

She drew in a deep breath and let it out. "I was thinking ... it might be a good idea to look for a house before ... before the baby comes."

"Before the—" Tony sat up and switched on the bedside lamp.

Her head now on the pillow, she squinted at him in the sudden glare of light. "Merry Christmas, Daddy."

"We're having a baby?" He drew her up and into his arms. "We're having a baby?"

"Uh-huh."

"When?"

"The end of July. Maybe early August."

Tony kissed her then, with all the sweetness, all the tenderness she had come to expect from his kisses.

Who could have thought her life would be so different today than it was when she arrived at this lodge one year ago, her heart wounded and unable to trust? Wishing for love but not daring to dream.

God thought it. That's who.

163

She smiled as she nestled into Tony's embrace and pondered the miracle of love.

Thank You, Jesus. And happy birthday.

ABOUT THE AUTHOR

Robin Lee Hatcher is the best-selling author of over seventy-five books. Her well-drawn characters and heartwarming stories of faith, courage, and love have earned her both critical acclaim and the devotion of readers. Her numerous awards include the Christy Award for Excellence in Christian Fiction, the RITA® Award for Best Inspirational Romance, Romantic Times Career Achievement Awards for Americana Romance and for Inspirational Fiction, the Carol Award, the 2011 Idahope Writer of the Year, and Lifetime Achievement Awards from both Romance Writers of America® (2001) and American Christian Fiction Writers (2014). *Catching Katie* was named one of the Best Books of 2004 by the Library Journal.

Learn more about Robin and her books by visiting her website and blog at www.robinleehatcher.com.

Goodreads

Pinterest

Bookbub

Newsletter sign-up

ALSO BY ROBIN LEE HATCHER

Stand Alone Titles

Here in Hart's Crossing

The Victory Club

Beyond the Shadows

Catching Katie

Whispers From Yesterday

The Shepherd's Voice

Ribbon of Years

Firstborn

The Forgiving Hour

Heart Rings

A Wish and a Prayer

When Love Blooms

A Carol for Christmas

Return to Me

Loving Libby

Wagered Heart

The Perfect Life

The Coming to America Series

Dear Lady

Patterns of Love

In His Arms

Promised to Me

Made in the USA
Monee, IL
22 April 2021

66521991R00095